## 3 Spine-tingling Tales for Young Readers

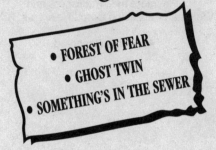

- FOREST OF FEAR
- GHOST TWIN
- SOMETHING'S IN THE SEWER

BARONET
BOOKS

Baronet Books, New York, New York

# FRIGHT TIME

### edited by
### Rochelle Larkin and Joshua Hanft

# FOREST OF FEAR

## by Anne Wolfe

**1**

If his pesky ten-year-old sister Allison didn't turn off her flashlight and get back to bed this minute, Mike Collins was going to clock her one. This is already the longest night of my life, he told himself, and it's only half over. It's quarter-to-one in the morning.

His darkened bedroom still smelled of popcorn and the nail polish that Allison had used earlier in the evening to paint their dog Herman's nails bright pink. Not only had she kept Mike from falling asleep by jumping up and down from her bed to the window, she had spilled popcorn all over the floor beside the bunk bed below his, where he was letting her stay just this once. But there was no use in being a nice guy by letting her sleep in his room after she'd had a nightmare, if she wasn't going to stay put. This was too much. A guy could go crazy.

From his bed in the corner, Herman let out a soft growl.

"You're even annoying Herman, Allie. How many times do I have to tell you to get away from the window." Mike sighed, thinking Allison in her pajamas looked like a purple-and-green Mexican jumping bean.

Pressed against the window, Allison gasped. "A star is falling down. Come here. Look."

Mike complied wearily, counting to ten under his breath to keep his cool. Just as he focused his gaze into the darkness outside, something bright appeared in the sky above the trees. The bright dot of light seemed to hang in the air for a second, then it streaked for the horizon, hovered another instant, and sank out of sight.

From a nearby bureau, Mike's digital clock started flashing.

"Whoops. Power surge."

"Where did that light thing go?" Allison asked.

Mike searched the sky frantically.

"Where is it?" Allison insisted.

"It must've been a plane having engine trouble," Mike said with authority. "Or it could've been a meteor."

"Can we go see it?" Allison asked.

"I didn't hear any crash. There's probably nothing to see."

"I don't think it was a meteor," Allison said stubbornly.

Herman barked once, rose from his bed, and joined them at the window, his tail wagging back and forth furiously.

"What is it, boy?"

Standing between them, the dog licked Mike's face, then Allison's, and raised a paw decked with neon pink nails toward the window pane.

Then Mike saw the red dot again, as it fanned out and fell beneath the tree line.

Just outside his family's small pasture fence, behind tall pine trees, the entire field glowed, bathed in the eerie red-orange light.

Mike rubbed the window pane with the sleeve of his pajama top, drying off the goo left by Herman's tongue. To get a better look, he opened the window. A blast of smoky air knocked him back a few steps. Allison clapped her hands over her nose and mouth. Herman barked and snapped his jaws open and shut at the sharp, hot draft of air.

Mike squinted against the bright light blazing in the distance. It was dimming slowly now. He listened as the family's small herd of horses and cows complained loudly from the pasture.

"Go get Mom and Dad," he said softly.

Allison whined, "No, you. I'm scared."

Then the blazing light went out completely. Suddenly, the pasture and surrounding field turned totally dark.

Mike leaned out the window and sniffed the darkness. A cloud of dust clogged his nose and burned in his throat. He turned away in a coughing fit, and recovered just in time to see Herman take a flying leap out the window.

"Dog!" he yelled. "Get back here now." Leaning as far out the window as he could, Mike shrieked, "Hermie!"

He pulled on a pair of jeans and lowered himself out the first-floor window to the ground below, determined to get the dog back into the house. Herman was a notorious runner. If given half a chance, he would chase deer for miles.

Beside him he felt a plop in the grass. Allison landed right beside him, holding her flashlight. He grabbed it out of her hand and sighed.

"Get back in the house, Allie. If you'd stayed still in the first place, Herman wouldn't be lost and I wouldn't be out here chasing him in the dark."

Allison folded her arms and pouted. "You were the one who opened the window."

Before he could lift his sister back up into his room, Allison walked into the woods saying, "Here, boy, here Hermie," and making kissing noises.

Mike stretched, coughed, and stood on the lawn with his head back. He could see only a sprinkling of stars between the tall tree branches—pine trees around the Collins's yard blocked out most of the sky.

If he hadn't been a nice guy and let Allison use his bunk, he'd be fast asleep beneath the covers. Now here he was in the middle of the night, about to chase after his sister and his dumb dog, who was probably in the next county by now.

He followed a short gravel path through the backyard and noticed the swings moving back and forth on Allison's swing set. Though the hot air was no longer blasting at the house, there was a definite breeze rustling the foliage toward the edge of the woods.

Being out there in the middle of the night gave him a pleasantly secret feeling. The sky was lighter against the black trees than he'd expected. There wasn't even a tiny glimmer of the red light anymore. The frogs peeping and the pine smell made the night air come alive, like magic. Stepping on the flattened trail into the woods where Allie and Herman had disappeared, he paused at the sound of a hoot owl.

Then he saw a faint red glow through the trees, and felt a tingle of excitement. The mysterious red light was too small and steady to be a fire.

For a moment, he wished he had told his parents before venturing out after Allie and Herman alone.

Pretending he was jogging the quarter-mile around the track at school, he took off after them, training the flashlight beam on the trail ahead of him. He could hear the dog barking, growling, and whining far ahead. Allison had totally disappeared.

Mike shouted and negotiated a steep bend in

the trail, where he almost fell over his sister. She was crouched down in a pile of leaves. He muttered, "Sorry," and dropped down beside her to catch his breath. Herman sat panting nearby, holding something in his mouth and offering his paw.

Allison grabbed the flashlight from Mike and took the dog's paw in one hand. "There's something yucky all over him." She looked the dog over from head to toe with the flashlight beam.

Herman dropped the thing in the grass, blinked into the light, and with a soft "woof" licked her face.

Bending down next to his sister, Mike touched and sniffed the dog's fur, then quickly turned his head away and coughed. "Gross. He smells like a cigarette."

Allison's voice trembled. "Is he burnt?"

"No." He really wasn't sure, but he didn't want to get his sister upset over the dog. Herman's eyes were bloodshot, bright red, and his whiskers were curled into tight wiry circles. His paws seemed smoky, and his body was hot to the touch. Gently, Mike patted the dog all over to check for sore spots. There were none.

He felt on the ground to find what Herman

had dropped, and picked up a shiny black mitt. It was made from sturdy light material. Turning it over, he noted the dog's fresh teeth marks in it.

"Looks like an oven mitt and feels like part of a garbage bag," he muttered. Gently, he poked his fingers into it and gasped. "There are three fingers!"

Allison moved in for a closer look. "Maybe it's something that goes on a cow."

"I don't think so." Mike turned it over in the light, holding it upside down, sideways, and turning it inside out. He stuffed it in the back pocket of his jeans.

"Come on, let's get back home."

Suddenly, Herman sprang to life and pulled the mitt out of Mike's pocket. He trotted ahead, looked back, barked, and went farther into the woods.

Allison ran after him with Mike right behind, over a maze of winding trails that seemed to go in circles.

"If we call for help, nobody will hear us," Mike muttered. "We have to go back now."

He caught up with Allison and grabbed her arm.

She tried to pull away. "No! I'm not leaving Herman."

Mike gave her arm a slight twist, just enough to stop her. "We have to go back!"

"Let me go!" Allison cried.

"No!" He resisted the impulse to yell at her. She was smaller and she was a girl. He wasn't about to lose his cool and have her rat on him. He gave her arm another tug.

Allison let out a bloodcurdling shriek that sent bats screeching from nearby trees. Without thinking, he dropped her arm and clapped both his hands over her mouth.

Then he smelled something. A chemical odor drifted over them and settled like a trap, filling his nostrils, head, and throat with a painful stench. Fearing he might barf on the spot, he pinched his nostrils shut and let Allison struggle to a standing position.

"Yeech. It smells like Daddy's feet." Allison covered her mouth and nose with both hands.

"Or yours," Mike muttered. "Let's get out of here."

"You think somebody died?" Allison asked, her voice trembling again. "And the corpse is out here rotting away?"

11

"I don't think so." Mike stood and peered through gaps in the trees, not entirely certain that Allison was wrong.

"Look!" Allison pointed skyward with the flashlight.

Across the black starry sky, a huge search-light scanned the clouds in large circles. An eerie, metallic humming sound echoed in the night.

"Get down!" Mike cried. "There's definitely something weird out here! Whatever it is, I don't think we should risk our necks trying to find out. Come on, Allie."

Mike picked his sister up, holding her up off the ground. She felt like she'd gained about a hundred pounds since the last time he tried to move her against her will. In two seconds, she managed to free herself.

"Bully!" she called over her shoulder, and ran deeper into the woods.

He heard her yelling, "Herman, here Herman," and moving farther away. "Yoo hoo. Where are you?"

An answering bark in the distant darkness told them the dog was way out of reach.

Mike kept his eyes on the searchlights and

called out, "He's hopeless. We have to go back. Come on."

Allison kept going. He could hear her slapping at branches that must have tangled up her long red hair. Mike ran after her, whacking his knee on a small tree and howling under his breath.

The searchlights moved in wider circles above them now, lighting the tops of nearby trees.

He moved cautiously in a crouch with his head down, peeking up at the searchlights every few seconds to avoid being caught in the glare.

The dog's barking seemed closer now, as if he was coming back to meet them. In a tiny clearing, Herman bounded out from behind a bush and jumped up in front of Mike, putting a paw on each shoulder, dropping the glove and washing Mike's face with his wet, leathery tongue.

"Phew. Get down." Mike wiped his nose and mouth. The smelly dog barked right in his face. "Okay, okay. What is it?"

The dog picked up the mitten and vanished into a clump of bushes and began barking furiously, hysterically, almost. Mike had never heard any dog bark like that in his life.

The searchlights moved lower, almost touch-

13

ing the ground around them.

"Whatever you do, stay out of sight. Don't let those searchlights catch you," Mike warned. "Not until we know what they are."

Allison grabbed his hand and followed. "You think those lights are from enemy spies?"

"I don't know. Whoever they are, I'm afraid Herman's going to find them and get himself dog-napped."

"No!" Allison insisted. "Hermie, wait up."

The cows and horses in the pasture were shrieking now, as they did when they were frightened. The creepy sound of the panicky animals brought chills to Mike's body, making him shiver all over.

Allison clung so tightly to him he could hardly walk.

"I feel icky," she whispered, holding her stomach with one hand.

"Don't you dare barf on me," Mike hissed.

"Somebody's watching us." Her voice quivered and became louder. "Somebody's touching me."

"Sssshh. It's just a bunch of straggly tree branches. If you keep yelling we'll get caught, so shush."

"It wasn't any tree branches. Somebody was

running fingers up and down my arm."

"You're imagining it."

Then Mike felt it. A strange sensation that things were crawling over his skin.

A high-pitched humming sound throbbed through his head, crackling like a damp power line.

"I feel it, too," he said.

She nodded and her lips quivered. Tears shone in her eyes.

"Why don't you go back home? I'll get the dog."

Allison rubbed her eyes and shrugged.

"You think you can find your way back home through the woods?" He doubted it.

She frowned and shrugged again.

His entire body was tingling now. His hands felt as if they were on backward. Little jabs poked him all over.

The air smelled like burning matches. Maybe something poisonous was invading the air. Like nerve gas. Chemical warfare. Invisible poisons used as weapons. Maybe Allison was right about enemy spies.

"My nose is running," Allison complained, "and I feel tired and stiff all over."

"Use your sleeve," Mike snapped, feeling her

body pull away from him.

She seemed stiff as a board all of a sudden. She fell face down in the dirt, her arms plastered against her sides, her legs straight as toothpicks.

"Allie! Get up! What's wrong?"

She didn't move or utter a sound.

"Come on, we've got to go back. I'll take you home now, I promise. Herman will find his way later on. Let's go."

She still didn't move.

He rolled her body over till she lay face up. Her eyes were frozen wide with fright. The expression on her face made him gasp and move away from her. She looked so scary he didn't want to touch her. She was sickly pale, and seemed cold to the touch.

The night air began to shimmer with heat.

He had to get them out of there.

# 2

He rubbed Allison's hands and face, trying to ignite a spark of life in her paralyzed body. He whispered wild promises in her ear, like, she could have the prize in every box of cereal for the next year, and he'd never cut the hair off her dolls again.

When he said she could have his new Space Cretins video game, she opened her eyes.

"I feel weird," she murmured.

"That's 'cause you are weird."

Allison sat up straight and glanced around as if she'd only just awakened from a nap. "What happened to me?"

Mike thought for a moment, his chest heaving. "You passed out. Like you were hypnotized or something." His voice shook. "I thought you were dead."

She searched his face as if she didn't believe him. Then she sat back and gazed at the sky.

"All I remember is you telling me to go home." She frowned. "Where's Herman? I want to go home now."

A blinding glare suddenly filled the area around them.

Mike held up his arms to shield his eyes. "They must've spotted us."

Allison's eyes bugged out. She began to shake all over.

"What's the matter?" Mike watched her arms

and legs tremble more violently every second. He clasped his hands over her knees to keep them still.

The air was heavy with a horrible stench.

Allison pointed to a dimly lit clearing far in front of them.

An oval silvery-white disk the size of a small house sent out thick black smoke from the four long stilts it stood on. On the underbelly were hundreds of tiny red lights.

Two creatures stood beneath the disk.

In the eerie blue-red spotlight, they were almost human looking as they crouched in the grass, digging furiously. Every few minutes they deposited mounds of dirt into a large bucket.

Allison opened her mouth wide to scream. No sound came out. Mike clapped his hands over her mouth to keep her quiet. She clawed at his hands and struggled against him, her muffled screams locked inside her.

The dog had totally disappeared, but Mike could swear he heard him whining from behind a nearby tree.

Fascinated and horrified, Mike tried to subdue Allison while he watched the creatures. They were all gray, without any body details.

They were simply gray outlines with goggle eyes like those on gas masks. They had no hair, mouths, noses, or ears that he could see. Just large heads, with those eyes, on short bodies, with arms and legs.

The three-fingered mitt probably belonged to one of them. He peered at the beings' hands and tried to count their fingers, but he was too far away.

A sudden sharp pain in his hand made him yelp. Before he knew what had happened, Allison managed to clench her teeth on his fingers.

As he pulled his hand away, she took another painful bite. Then, without Mike's being able to stop her, she opened her mouth wide and screamed at the top of her lungs.

Her bloodcurdling scream brought Herman back to them, shivering, his tail between his legs. Timidly, he jumped up on Allison and licked her face.

"Quiet!" Mike hissed. His knees trembled so hard beneath him, he was sure he heard them knocking together. Or maybe it was Allison's teeth chattering. "I don't know what's going on, or who those people are. All I know is we have to get out of here!"

Allison was now screaming soundlessly, pointing to the strange creatures, who had stopped digging to peer through the trees in their direction.

"They—they—what are they?" Allison stammered. She shook with fright.

"I don't know, but they saw us now, thanks to you." Mike put his hands on Allison's shoulders to keep her from bolting into the bright blue-red light a hundred yards away.

"Now keep quiet and do as I say. I'll grab Herman by the collar. We'll turn around, stay close together, and run all the way back home. Got it?"

Allison sniffed. Herman whimpered and lifted his leg against a tree.

"Okay, I'm counting to three and then we run." He grabbed Herman's collar. "Get ready, get set..."

Herman struggled against his grip. Allison turned her body toward home and waited for him to give the signal.

"One...two..."

"Woof!"

"Herman, sshhhh!"

"Woof! Woof!"

"Three!"

Herman shot ahead of them, yelping. Mike lost his grip on the dog's collar. Branches crackled behind them. Allison darted after the dog.

"So much for togetherness," Mike muttered as his sister and their dog disappeared into the dark woods.

## 3

Mike peeked over his shoulder toward the creatures. They were only a hundred feet away from him now, headed his way and gaining quickly.

Their feet didn't seem to touch the ground.

"Allie, runnnnn!" Mike tore through the trees in a panic, not sure of his direction, hoping he could catch up with Allie and the dog and find their way home. But Allison and Herman were out of sight. Stumbling, feeling branches tearing the skin on his arms and face, Mike pushed himself in a blind panic over fallen logs, through puddles, smacking himself on wayward bushes as he ran into total darkness.

He tucked his arms in closer to his body and doubled his speed. Gasping for air, his heart pounded against his chest. His leg muscles cramped and burned so bad he wanted to fall down, but he pushed himself to get farther away from them. I'm being chased by space creatures from a UFO. And if they're not Ufonauts, they're enemy spies, right here in New Jersey, using chemical weapons, he thought.

He thought he heard them chattering right behind him now, squawking like geese, their inhuman sounds punctuated by little beeps.

Still running breathlessly, he noticed something was happening to him. Every time they beeped his pain went away a little bit. He listened, waited for the next beep, and the next. As each beep came, he felt calmer and lighter all over.

Almost before he knew it, he was floating over the ground. The beeps kept him up, letting him nearly fly. He gave in to the feeling, and let it carry him. He began to enjoy the sensation of flying. He felt light, and his chest swelled with awe at being airborne.

Suddenly, he felt sleepy. He closed his eyes and fell into a dream that he was flying over the trees, into the clouds, his entire body filled with warm white light, his head filled with music.

He wanted to go on feeling that way forever, but a long loud "Mooooo!" cut into his trance. He struggled, against the warm drowsy feeling, to remain alert.

He knew what that sound meant. They'd gotten one of the cows.

Suddenly, his body gained a new heaviness. He fell from the treetops, and landed with a thump on the woody ground below. He shook his head, feeling totally out of it. He knew he should be running. The creatures would surely catch him now!

But he couldn't seem to move.

On the ground, he curled up into a ball with his eyes closed and waited.

Nothing happened.

Fearfully, he stood up and slowly looked around, his eyes straining to see into the glowing red smoke that filled the darkness.

The two strange creatures that had been chasing him were now turning away.

He watched them approach a third creature standing in the reddish light below their craft. He turned to run away. Then he noticed something else in the red light.

Aggie, Mike's favorite cow, stood beside the

third creature. And now she was into the air toward the belly of the ship, bawling loudly.

"Aggie, no!" Mike stood helplessly and watched his cow disappear into the ship. "Give her back! Leave her alone!"

Tears sprang to his eyes and a lump formed in his throat. His arms and legs began to quake, not from fear, but from anger. His hands balled into tight fists. They had no right to steal his favorite cow, the pet he had raised from a tiny calf.

The last thing he heard before Aggie disappeared into the ship was the faint tinkling sound of her bell.

He ran for the spacecraft, picking up large rocks along the way until he had his arms totally full. When he reached the right distance from the silvery oval, he dropped the rocks at his feet and, one by one, heaved them at the glistening craft. Each one struck the side of the ship with a metallic crunch and bounced right off as if the rocks were rubber balls.

The long silver legs of the spacecraft began to retract into its bottom. Then the craft hovered and slowly moved, crashing down small trees in its path. About a hundred yards away, it settled down again on its red-lit stilts.

"Let go of my cow!" Mike yelled. "Whoever you are, this is private property! Go home!" The family's remaining herd bellowed in the distant pasture. Of all the cows, why did they have to take Aggie? If they needed a cow so badly, they could've taken any of the others.

He felt a soft, deep blow to his stomach. Next thing he knew, he was flat on his back on the ground, with all the wind knocked out of him.

He tried to sit up. A strong force pressed down against his shoulders.

He wished he had a white handkerchief to wave. He heard his own voice tremble and say, "Don't shoot. I surrender."

He struggled beneath the heavy force that kept pushing him down. But as soon as he stopped resisting, his body rose back up into the air.

*What was happening?*

He kicked and grabbed at branches. From high up in the sky, he floated above the trees and saw the twinkling lights of the entire town arranged before him like a Christmas display.

Could nerve gas make you fly?

The awesomeness of it brought tears to his eyes. He remembered lying on the roof of his house only three days before to watch the sun set in orange and red colors so bright it hurt to stare at them. Now here he was, floating in the empty sky, gazing at diamond lights all around him. Suddenly, he wondered if he had died and gone to heaven.

How long could he float around up here before he came crashing down to earth and broke every bone in his body?

Rolling, floating, then swimming, his body moved through the air toward the spacecraft. He was unable to change direction. It was pulling him to it. Closer and closer he drifted, down into the trees until he was level with the disk's tiny round windows. Peering inside, he saw one of the creatures at a large table in what looked like a hospital operating room. Then in a flash, he dropped down a few feet and found himself face to face with the wall of dull gray metal that was the disk. He stretched out his hand to touch it, but it almost seemed to move away, though he couldn't see that it had actually budged.

Inside his head, a buzzing began, slow and soft, then louder and louder until it hurt. The buzzing and the overpowering smell of burning rubber made him feel sick to his stomach.

He was still suspended in the air.

*This isn't real.*

He tensed his entire body, ready to fall to the ground. He raced downward, out of control, and watched the stars above rush farther away.

He expected to hear his bones crack, waited for the ear-splitting crash into the ground.

It never came.

He realized he wasn't moving anymore. He had landed without hurting himself. He felt dirt, weeds, and rocky ground. He stood up, weak in the knees, and a wave of nausea overpowered him. He staggered and tried to walk away.

Suddenly, a whirling, howling draft grabbed him and carried him up, up, up, toward the glaring white-red warmth. And into the spaceship.

# 4

The strange darkness inside paralyzed him. Then he jerked, twisted, and slipped around helplessly, finally sinking into what he thought must be a wall. He crouched on all fours. His head touched a cool, soft floor.

Darkness. There was nothing but darkness.

He wondered if he'd gone blind. But as his eyes adjusted, he saw dark gray shadows that made him imagine a gang of ghosts stood ready to pounce at him. Then he wondered why it was dark, and if they were going to brainwash him.

A loud metallic whine began, and the darkness vibrated. The sound reminded him of a giant dentist's drill. He curled into a ball, closed his eyes, and shivered from head to toe.

The room suddenly blazed with light. He felt the presence of something in front of him. Opening one eye, he saw what looked like the webbed foot of a giant duck.

A creature stood before him, not much bigger than he was, but to his mind, it was larger than the most humongous giant on earth.

Mike inhaled deeply. Then, jumping up like an angry lion he roared and wailed, striking out at it with his fists.

"Enemy spy!" he shouted.

The creature jumped back with a high-pitched squawk. Its three-fingered hand closed over Mike's shoulders, but he felt nothing.

"Let me go! And my cow, too! Let us go, please!"

He saw its large black slanted eyes. And suddenly he felt cornered, like the tiny rabbit he had caught the month before. It had hidden behind a skinny little bush, thinking it was safe. Mike had pounced on it and thrown his Red Sox cap over it too, and then let it go. Maybe this creature would let him go, too.

Was it trying to tell him something? He saw something move in the creature's face. Thin lips that only showed when they moved.

It looked at him. Mike felt rather than heard it tell him, "Stay there. Just stay there."

Suddenly his own words pounded inside his head. I must get out of here! Out! Now!

He focused on the creature's eyes. He'd never seen eyes like these before. They changed shape from slanted to round and back.

Those eyes were suddenly inside his brain!

This is a dream. I can wake up. Please, let me wake up.

If this wasn't a dream, who were they? Were they space pirates? They stole Aggie. What did they want from him? He didn't have any money. He didn't have anything. What *could* they want? He stared at the creature.

The eyes were still there, telling him to stay put. The eyes talked to him. It was the eyes that talked, that pounded inside his head till they seemed to have no connection to a body. They were just *eyes*.

Then he decided he knew what the creatures were: Air Force test pilots on a secret mission, so secret they dressed in uniforms, where only their eyes showed. Maybe he didn't have to be afraid.

But he was!

The eyes pressed in closer against his eyes. They shone into him and through him like X-rays. He was sure they had the power to reduce him to a pile of flesh and bones, to burn the insides right out of him.

While the eyes bore into him, he was suspended, floating.

They were messing with his mind!

He wanted to go home.

What if he couldn't? What if he could never go home again? What if they took him away with them to some distant star?

"I want to go home." Mike finally found the words and said them out loud to the creature.

The creature drew back its eyes, retreated and cocked its head as if trying to understand what Mike had just said. It looked at him for a long time. His gaze on Mike made him feel totally numb.

Then it tried to move him.

Though its hands were on him, Mike felt no pressure. His body seemed to float with the creature's touch. Even though Mike resisted, dragging his feet across the floor and twisting his body every which way, he was moving under this alien power.

It helped him into a metal chair like an electric chair he'd seen in a prison movie. Leathery straps hung from the chair's arms and front legs.

"Please, please let this be only a dream," he pleaded loudly.

The creature seemed puzzled and put its head close to his again, eyes to eyes.

Mike waited.

Then it strapped him in, binding his arms and legs.

He decided to keep his eyes closed. Over and over he repeated to himself, Keep your eyes closed. Don't open them.

He was powerless now, strapped into the chair. He knew the creature was still there. But as long as everything was black, and his eyes were closed, he didn't have to believe it was there.

He didn't have to *believe* anything. He could believe he was somewhere else.

He imagined himself walking quickly through the woods, leading Aggie safely back into the pasture. He opened the gate, scratched her in her favorite place between the eyes, smacked her rump, and closed the gate behind her. Then he headed for home. He dreamed of his room, that Herman would be there waiting, pink nails and all. His mother would make chocolate chip pancakes with whipped cream for breakfast, and let him drink a bottle of cola with it instead of orange juice. He'd play Space Cretins all day and win every game.

Then he realized the creature was there by his side. He had that feeling it was holding him, though he couldn't really feel it. He just felt as if he was floating again, suspended in air.

Suddenly he wanted to *see* it.

He opened his eyes a crack. It was gone.

He squinted in the bluish light that sparkled all around him. A tiny blue hospital operating room surrounded him, with operating table, utensils, and strange machines built into the walls. Everything was spotlessly clean. The circular room had one tiny window.

He was still strapped down, with his feet dangling over the edge.

He closed his eyes and remembered his tonsillectomy five years before. Straining his mind to go back to that hospital, he willed himself farther and farther away from his surroundings. Still back there in his mind, he imagined himself unbuckling the straps, getting free, and walking toward the wall, guided only by his instincts, keeping his eyes closed. But it was no use.

"Let me out!" His loud voice echoed off the circular walls.

He felt sick to his stomach. If he had to throw up, there was no place to do it. He moaned.

Glancing up toward the ceiling, he noticed a tiny viewing screen, like a television monitor. In it, he saw Aggie on a chain in a tiny rectangular room standing alone, head down, sniffing the floor.

He shouted as if she could hear. "Here, girl. Hey, Aggie-Waggie." He pulled against the straps, trying unsuccessfully to free his hands. If only he had a fistful of sugar, he thought he could lure her away, get her off the ship and back to the pasture. He watched Aggie raise her head briefly and then let it drop.

He cried, "Don't worry, girl. This is just a silly joke. Those men are test pilots dressed as Martians, and when they're done with this top secret mission of theirs, we'll go home."

For a moment he almost believed it.

Aggie couldn't hear him. Her image vanished. He hit his hand against the table, frustrated. He blinked and squinted at the monitor, but she was no longer there.

He remembered finding her three years ago as a spindly-legged calf standing in the barn with a huge red bow around her neck. She was his birthday present. His father promised she could be his pet, unlike the other cows he raised to give milk or beef. Mike never understood why his father kept cows anyway, living on a stretch of 20 acres in the Jersey suburbs, when they could buy all the milk and beef they wanted at the supermarket.

Aggie was always special. She ran after Mike in the pasture and licked his face when he finished feeding her, as if kissing him good-bye. In the winter, the dog kept Aggie company in the barn. Herman liked to curl up against her in the hay.

Mike sighed. He'd give anything to be back home in the barn, watching Aggie and Herman snuggle against each other.

Instead, he was trapped in a nightmare that wouldn't quit.

It only got worse.

# 5

Two creatures stood squawking over him.

They had odd-shaped heads with large skulls that narrowed to pointy chins. Their vacant, almond-shaped eyes reached around the sides of their heads. Mike wondered if they could see things all around them. Their skin was bluish-gray and they had no hair.

Their body movements were stiff, like robots.

One of the gray featureless creatures pushed up Mike's sleeve, and the two looked at his arm, turning it over curiously. They pushed over a machine with a big lens and took a picture of his arm.

Still squawking to each other, they took turns peering into the machine. One of them rotated the machine over to focus on his own arm and peered in, then turned it back to Mike's, as if comparing their skins.

The creature put on a black mitt like the one Hermie had found. Then the real horror began.

A knifelike tool emerged from somewhere.

"Don't come near me with that thing!" Mike screamed.

The creature ignored him, as if he didn't understand or hear him. The knife scraped flakes of skin from his arm. The creature put the flakes on something like a clear plastic slide, which he rolled up and filed away in a drawer.

The light in the room changed suddenly to a broad band of orange, yellow and white. The creatures unstrapped him and moved his body onto a huge slab made of crystal. He expected it to be cold, like a block of ice, but it was warm.

Then, waving a long thin tube of crystal in the air over his head, a creature shot light into his chest. Looking like a laser from his Space Cretins video game, the light made a small crackling sound, like the bug-zapper in the backyard at home.

"What are you doing to me?" Mike cried. "I want to go home!"

The light felt like a needle! With its extended

beam, it looked to him like a long needle, and it stung. More than anything, he wanted to scratch the place where the light was touching him. It began to itch and burn like crazy. Suddenly his entire body felt bloated and tight, as if his skin was being stretched out from the inside.

The room went suddenly dark.

But something was still glowing. That something was him! He glanced down at his body and saw the outline of his entire skeleton etched in bright red light. His bones sparkled like a Halloween costume.

He screamed until he thought his lungs would burst.

His screaming seemed to throw them into a panic. The lights blazed on and the creatures squawked in confusion. But they didn't turn off the needle. It bored into Mike like a bee sting that wouldn't quit.

"Turn it off! Turn if off!" he screamed. His body was fastened to the crystal table and he couldn't twist himself away from the needle. "Let me go! Get me out of here!"

His head felt thick, as if it had been stuffed with cotton. His thoughts could hardly circulate in his brain. But the same panicky thoughts surfaced over and over again. Where's Allison? Is she all right? Is Herman okay? I should've stayed with them to make sure they got home safe. Will I ever go home again? Will I see my mom and dad?

Then a creature cut off a lock of his hair, wrapped it up, and filed it away.

They took off his sneakers and looked at his feet.

He kept his eyes shut as much as he could.

One of them took something from beneath his toenail, and cut some of his nail, then they both felt his feet all over.

One unbuttoned his pajama shirt and he felt the touch of many tiny little needles, stinging like cat claws, on his chest.

"What are you doing?" Mike resisted the tears that burned in his eyes. More than anything, he didn't want to be a crybaby. But he had no idea why they were doing these things to him.

A third creature joined the other two. The new creature studied him. It stepped forward and waved his hand over Mike's chest. The stinging faded away. For a moment he felt relaxed and grateful to the creature for stopping the pain. This creature was slightly different than the others, about six inches shorter and thinner. Mike wondered if it was a child, if these creatures brought their children on this strange mission.

Then it spoke inside his head.

"Do not be afraid."

He felt a rush of warmth through his body. And suddenly, wanting to shake its hand, he lifted his arm toward the creature. It glanced back at the others. Their backs were turned and they seemed to be conferring about something. After a moment's hesitation, it clasped his hand and held on tightly.

Mike smiled and looked at its eyes, waiting for its eyes to press in on his again.

"Who are you? Can you help me?" he softly whispered.

Instead of feeling as if an X-ray was boring into him, Mike saw in its eyes an aerial view of a strange landscape of grays, browns, and pale blues, dotted with metallic structures. The landscape was totally flat and the horizon was dusty gray and sunless.

A strange planet? Or future Earth?

In Mike's mind, a voice said, "My Earth name is Josiah. Do you really know anything at all about the universe?"

39

Mike strained to recall the astronomy lesson he'd had at the end of seventh grade. "No, except the sun is the center of the solar system. There are nine planets. And millions of stars."

The creature made a strange honking sound. Mike guessed that Josiah was laughing at him.

The other two creatures in the room turned back toward Josiah and squawked at him. Josiah stepped away from the table, and Mike's warm feeling faded.

There was something about the two creatures that deeply frightened Mike. They looked and moved differently than Josiah. For one thing, their eyes were vacant and they seemed to have no feelings. He didn't feel safe with them at all.

"Who are you?" he yelled. "What do you want?"

The larger two put their tiny hands to their ears, as if his shouting was painful to them. They put their heads together a moment and squawked at Josiah, then left the room. Josiah stayed behind.

Mike's chest felt cold. He strained against the straps, trying unsuccessfully to button up his pajama shirt.

Turning to an opening in the wall, Josiah produced a map, much wider than it was long, filled with little dots. Some were pin points and others were big as quarters. There were curved lines and circles connecting the dots. Josiah pointed to a series of dotted lines.

"Is that how you get to your top secret air base?" Mike asked.

Josiah shook his head. "No. That is the route to you."

"From where? Where are you from?"

"Fabrian."

"Is that a planet?"

"A distant star."

*Yeah, sure.* If this was a game, he had no choice but to play along. "How old are you?" Mike asked.

"What is old?" Josiah suddenly cocked his head inquisitively.

"How many years? You know, your age..." Mike shrugged, unable to put it into other words.

"How many years?" Josiah repeated the question to himself.

"You know, years. It has something to do with the earth revolving around the sun, and the rotation of the earth, and the seasons, and stuff."

Mike shook his arm that held his watch. "Every time the hands turn around this dial it's 12 hours."

Josiah clearly did not understand.

Mike stared at him a moment and asked, "What are you? Are you, like, from the future? Or are you some kind of Martians? And why did you take my cow?"

Josiah stared. "For your food. Do you not eat your cow?" Josiah scratched his bald head.

"No. You can't either. She's not for eating. She's my friend."

"Friend."

"She is part of my family. She makes me feel... good. In here." He pulled one hand toward his heart but the strap wouldn't reach.

Josiah touched Mike's chest. "In there."

Mike nodded.

Josiah pulled his three-fingered hand away suddenly.

"No, it's okay. It's good." Mike willed him to understand. "It's good."

"Are all your worries in there, too?" Josiah asked.

Mike shook his head.

"Where are they?"

Mike touched his head against Josiah's hand. "In here. I think all my worries are in my head."

Josiah's thin lips formed an O. "It is so big. You must have many in there."

Mike laughed. "I worry about not getting out of here," he said, his words flowing out in a torrent, "and I worry about if I do get out of here." He gasped for breath, feeling suddenly agitated. "If I do get out of here, nobody will believe me. Nobody will believe I saw you, that I was up here, or anything. Why are you doing this to me? Everybody will think I'm crazy."

"No, we are going to take you away."

"What do you mean? You can't. Who's going to take me away?"

"Those other two. We are all Fabrians. We have orders to bring back specimens."

"I don't understand." Mike lay down and stared at the ceiling, hoping Josiah's words didn't mean what he thought they did. In a hushed voice he whispered, "Can't you make them let me go?"

"I am hybrid. I have no power."

"A hybrid?" Mike thought of the flowers in his mother's garden, the ones that were produced by mixing two different types. She said they were

43

hybrids. Was Josiah a mixture of some kind?

"What do you mean? You have more power than the other two. You can talk to me and they can't. You're good and they're not."

"I am nothing because I am only half Fabrian. And part human."

Mike blinked, open-mouthed.

"Hybrids are all nothings, empty, like shells. We work. That is all we do. We are nothing."

"No. Maybe the Fabrians tell you that, but it's a lie. You're something. You're different. You're good."

Josiah's eyes dimmed. "The Fabrians are a dying breed. Humans are hearty. The Fabrians must have more strength to prolong their species. But only full-blooded true Fabrians have power."

"Why do you need to steal humans? Why not leave us here, why not let me go home?" Mike felt like a lab experiment, like the preserved frog he'd had to dissect in Biology. "This is crazy. You can't take me away. I can't just disappear like a magician's rabbit. My parents will miss me."

"Yes, it is clear that you have meaning to others here on Earth, that you are something here," Josiah said.

"Yeah. That's why I have to go home. That's why I belong out there, not in here. But I can't even get off this table until somebody opens these straps."

"You will fight," Josiah said with a hint of quiet admiration.

Josiah's words surprised him. He thought a moment. "How can I fight? There's two of them, plus you, and only one of me. You can do things with your minds, make me move, use some kind of chemical warfare against me, and if I try to hurt them the others will stop me."

Josiah rested his hand next to Mike's. Mike gently touched the grayish skin. It felt like plastic. The skin was hard. The fingertips were firm.

Mike looked closely at the skin covering Josiah's body. It was loose and folded in places, like a form-fitting uniform. Unlike the others' straight narrow chests, Josiah's chest was sturdy looking, as if he were muscular and powerfully built. How could he have no power?

Suddenly it dawned on him. There were different kinds of power. Muscle power and brain power. Despite what Josiah said, the true Fabrians seemed to have neither of those. Their only real power was in their advanced technology.

Mike hadn't really tapped his own power against them, especially his brain power. He had let them take him physically, had allowed them to invade his mind. Was it possible he could at all resist?

Just as he had allowed them to manipulate him, could he decide not to allow them?

If he applied all his brain power to the situation, his physical power just might give the Fabrians a real challenge, too, something they might never have encountered before from wimpy human kids like himself.

"You can help me escape," Mike said. "And by the time I leave, you might realize you're something, and you will know where real power comes from!"

"You just think you have no power. They made you believe it so *they* could have power over you," Mike said, guessing that the Fabrians treated Josiah like a servant.

Josiah's eyes brightened like two giant tear-shaped marbles. His shoulders straightened and his pointed chin tilted out slightly.

"You have the power to help me escape. Together we can use our brains against the others. If we do, I can get away from here before this ship takes off." Mike looked for a sign that Josiah might agree to help him, but the Fabrian stood motionless, without changing his expression at all.

Suddenly, the creature glanced around, his gaze resting on two sets of belts and handles fastened to the wall. He seemed confused for a moment. Then a loud, high-pitched roar shook the room. A sound like exploding bombs rocked the table. Mike gripped its edges to stay centered so the table wouldn't fall over with him on it.

In a mechanical voice, Josiah recited, "We must prepare to leave."

"No! We can't! You can't let them take me away!" Mike's breath came in short gasps. "We have to do something. We have to use our brains to get me out. We have to think of one single thing, *escape*, and nothing else. Just getting me out."

Josiah cocked his head at Mike. Without explanation, he unfastened the straps on Mike's arms and legs. Mike sat up, rubbing the sore places where the straps had burned into his skin. He turned to Josiah. Somehow, he had to make this alien become his friend. He had to show him that he had power—and he had to make him use that power to help Mike escape.

"We both have to share the same thought. We have to pour every ounce of brain energy we have into that thought. The energy will make it come true, make it come alive." Mike put all the strength he still had into his words.

"Concentrate." Mike counted to three and took deep breaths so he could think clearly. He hoped that Josiah understood him, that he knew what it meant to concentrate on something. Josiah had to understand. He *had* to. It was the only way Mike could make it out of there.

"Concentrate on setting me free, on leaving me behind before you take off for Fabrian. See me on the ground. See me happy, safe at home, anywhere, just see me back on earth! Can you do that?" he pleaded.

Josiah stared at him. He didn't understand. Mike might just as well have been talking to a brick wall.

"Please, Josiah. You have to understand me." He gazed deep into the creature's eyes and hollered in his mind, *You do understand me*!

Then a strange sensation came over him, as if Josiah's mind was joining his in a single unit. A larger, more powerful unit.

The spacecraft rocked gently. Mike felt the legs retract beneath them, just as he'd felt the landing gear retract in an airplane many times before. A soft whirring sound, then metallic click, and the craft felt as if it was airborne. *We're taking off*!

He remembered his best game of Space Cretins, when the meteors bombarded the demon ships one after another, and forced them to crash back down to Earth. He strained his brain to picture a force that would push the spacecraft back onto the ground. Imagining two mighty hands, in his mind he saw the ship rev its engines against an outside force just above the trees. Bracing himself flat against the wall, he waited for the craft to sputter and lose power.

This had to work. It had to.

Nothing changed. The craft picked up speed. It was high in the air. Mike ran to the small round window. He saw his town far below, like a necklace made of teeny dots of light.

He ran to the wall and pounded on the knobs

and levers of the built-in machinery. As he pushed buttons, he set off all sorts of things. A pair of robot hands sprang from a cabinet and clawed the air. A loud hissing noise came from some sort of chemical spraying the room.

Josiah let out an eerie high-pitched squawk.

"I don't care if this kills us all," Mike hollered, coughing and choking. "If I can't go back home, I don't want to go anywhere!"

Josiah squawked again and shielded his eyes with his hands. "You do not know what you are doing. That is harmful to you! We must seal the room immediately!"

# 7

He woke to Josiah's eyes against his. Josiah's hands pressed against his chest. Warmth and strength flooded through his body, filling him like an inflated tire, pumping him full of— power.

He got up and searched frantically through the gassy fog, looking for the door. He was going to run through it, but Josiah helped him float through. Together they left the room. Josiah sealed the room behind them.

Even now that he was outside, Mike still felt dizzy and nauseated.

"I'm going to be sick," he moaned.

Josiah passed his hand over Mike's chest. The nausea went away.

"Thanks. Don't say you have no power. You've got enough for both of us." Mike smiled at his new friend.

Josiah pointed to Mike's chest. "Am I still in there?"

Mike laughed and put his hand over his heart. "Yes. You're here."

Josiah brought him to a porthole-shaped window in the circular corridor. Together, they watched as the earth became a large round mass below. Stars twinkled as they moved past the window.

"It's too late." Mike felt a lump form in his throat. "I'm a prisoner. I'll never go home again."

No. He couldn't afford to think that. He would not surrender to them, no way, nohow, never! He would fight to the very end. If he had to, he would die trying to get back home.

"Keep concentrating, Josiah," he said, trying to keep the panic out of his voice. "Keep thinking of returning me to Earth right now, and there won't be any more trouble."

Josiah backed away against the wall.

Then Mike felt his mind joining Josiah's. He imagined their two minds forming a heavy steel bar that nothing else could penetrate.

Without a word, Josiah moved to a sliding panel in the wall and pushed a button.

The metallic roar of the spacecraft's engines stopped abruptly. A deathly stillness filled the air. Then suddenly, the craft tilted sideways and began to fall.

Mike's head nearly hit the ceiling as the rapid drop threw him up off the floor and bounced him around like a Ping-Pong ball.

Josiah grabbed onto a handle near the window. Reaching out for Mike, he took his arm and held fast, pulling him to the side wall and holding him as steady as he could.

Mike hugged Josiah. "What's happening?" he asked. As if to answer him, a screeching alarm sounded throughout the ship.

Mike heard a crackling sound in the corridor. Blue-black smoke billowed from one corner.

The scary sound of metal scraping on metal echoed everywhere. The ship shuddered violently and continued to fall.

Able to peek out the window now, Mike saw the earth hurtling toward them.

"We're going to crash!" he screamed.

Josiah hugged him tightly. The creature felt soft, squishy, as if he were made out of cookie dough. His giant eyes were closed, leaving his face totally empty of any features.

Suddenly Mike felt safe. Josiah would take care of him, he knew that somehow. If he could only get through the crash landing, he might have a chance...

"You *do* have power," he said to Josiah. "You reversed the ship!"

Josiah opened his eyes. They sparkled brightly again. Amidst the shivering and quaking, he made Mike feel that he was on his side.

But nothing prepared Mike for the horrible sound of metal slamming into the earth.

It was a zillion times worse than the sound inside a plane bouncing off thunderclouds. Pieces of steel hurled like missiles over his head and bounced off his stomach, making him double over, gasping for air.

After rocking with a high-pitched metallic whine, the craft seemed to settle and hum, sputtering now and then. A cloud of blue smoke snaked across the ceiling of the round corridor.

Mike sat gasping. He looked at Josiah. To his shock, the little Fabrian was unconscious beneath a panel that had pulled loose from the wall.

"Josiah!" Mike gingerly touched the creature's arm with his hand. "Josiah!" He heard the hysteria in his voice.

Inside his mind a small voice said, "Run!"

Mike stood over Josiah and watched for signs that he was regaining consciousness. He could hear the other two Fabrians squawking in a distant room. He expected them to come running, to check out the escaping smoke, to see if Josiah was okay, at least. But they didn't appear.

Again, a small voice hissed, "Run!"

He couldn't.

He bent down over Josiah and gently moved the silver panel, which seemed weightless, in spite of its effect on the small Fabrian.

"Fight, Josiah, find your power," he whispered again.

He held his hand to Josiah's chest and took a deep breath, thinking, I will my power into you. All my power is yours.

Josiah's huge eyes stared blankly toward the ceiling. Mike passed a hand over them. There was no movement, no brightness. Josiah's eyes were black empty pools.

Power. Power. Power.

Nothing. Josiah lay still. Mike pressed a firm finger into the skin of his arm. It remained indented.

"No! Wake up!" Mike cried.

For sure, the others would come now. Come to get him. He didn't care. All he could think of was that Josiah was hurt. Hurt trying to help *him*.

It was his fault.

A tear rolled down his cheek . It dropped onto Josiah's face. Then another and another. Crybaby, Mike scolded himself. I wish I were home in my room fast asleep right now, with Allie and Herman. I wish all this had never happened, that this giant hunk of tin had never landed next to our pasture, that everything could be just as it was before, that this would be just a nightmare and that I'd wake up right now this minute . . .

The smoke was clearing, but he could hardly breathe.

Then he saw a dot of light in Josiah's eyes.

Slowly, the dot widened, and glowed like a burning candle.

Again, the voice cried, "Run!"

"Save yourself," Josiah's voice said inside his head.

"What about you?" Mike pleaded.

Josiah's eyes blinked once. He pointed to Mike's chest. "I will be in there always."

"No. Come home with me. You can meet my parents, my dog, and my sister Allison, if you have a strong stomach."

"Who's this Allison you talk about?" Josiah asked. His body didn't move.

Mike clamped his mouth shut. He didn't want to speak of his family any more, afraid he'd put them in danger. He prayed Allison had gotten home, that she had awakened his parents, that the police were on their way after everyone heard the huge crash. *The entire world must've heard them crash!*

He strained to hear sirens from somewhere outside the ship, but all he heard was a monotonous metallic hum, like the sound made by their refrigerator at home.

Josiah managed to stand up then. Stiffly and silently he held up his hand. On the middle finger was a shiny copper band with a clear glass stone. Josiah slipped off the ring and held it out to Mike. Mike put his own finger through it. The ring was too small and rested just above his knuckle.

"When you return home, show them this," Josiah said. "They will believe you."

Mike looked the ring. Unlike the ones he'd seen in stores, Josiah's ring radiated a unique magic all its own.

"Don't let the other Fabrians see it," Josiah said. "They will want you to forget all about what has happened."

"I won't forget about it. They can never, never make me forget. I'll remember this if it's the last thing I ever remember!"

Sadly, Josiah said, "I hope you don't remember. It will be better for you if you forget all about this."

Mike hugged the ring to his chest. "I won't. We have books and movies about things like this. Other people have remembered. They call these 'close encounters'."

"What do other humans say about us?" Josiah asked.

"I don't know. Usually not much. I don't think many people actually get this far, I mean, not many get to meet you face to face. Mostly, a lot of people just see UFOs."

"What are UFOs?"

"Strange things in the sky, 'unidentified flying objects', your ship, stuff like that."

Suddenly Josiah turned around and squawked. The other two Fabrians stood in the doorway. Mike felt their anger radiate right through him. He froze.

Josiah stood with his hands behind his back, his large eyes looking down at the floor.

Rushing at Mike, the two creatures pushed him back into the partially-destroyed operating room and made him lie flat on a table. One of them pushed Josiah out into the corridor. The other bound Mike's arms and legs.

Mike yelled, "Don't leave me, Josiah! Please!"

Out of sight beyond the doorway, Josiah merely squawked in reply.

The larger creature spotted Josiah's ring on Mike's finger. With an ear-splitting squawk, he grabbed Mike's finger and pulled.

Mike kicked, pushed, pulled, punched, shouted, and twisted against the leather straps. Letting his body go wild, he felt a wave of strength wash over him. He was sure it came from the ring. He knew it would help him do whatever he needed to get out of there.

The first arm strap finally broke. With his right hand free, he managed to undo the left while keeping the Fabrians away with punches and body twists. With both hands free, he undid his feet, which wasn't easy. The straps wrapped around his ankles and his calves, and when he tried to tear them apart they tangled in knots.

From the corner of his eye he saw Josiah peeking into the room. He felt Josiah helping him, somehow, sending him more strength to keep fighting. His leg straps popped off and he leaped down from the table. Turning it on its side, he used it as a barrier between himself and the two confused creatures fiddling with a broken machine attached to the wall.

A loud beeping noise shrieked throughout the craft, reminding Mike of a car alarm. It was the same beeping noise that had paralyzed him and allowed them to capture him in the first place.

He wasn't about to let it stop him again.

Josiah's words shouted in his head, "Fight it. Close your mind to the beeps. Close it now. Think against it, keep moving."

Mike rubbed the ring and made sure it was secure on his finger. Then he focused on his fists. Using them as weapons, he punched and pounded his way out of the room into the corridor. There were scuffling noises behind him. With a loud yell, he drowned out the beeps that bounced from wall to wall, threatening to take over his mind.

If he could only find the door, if he could only remember how he'd gotten in there, but he couldn't. The darn beeps had him mesmerized. He couldn't remember a thing. But he had to find his way out.

Why were they chasing him? Why didn't they just let him go? They'd gotten a chance to examine him. It must be the ring. They didn't want him to have it. They didn't want him to have proof that he'd been there.

If he turned around and gave them the ring, they'd probably let him go.

He wanted it more than anything now.

The creatures floated over the shiny floor, squawking to each other, following him at a safe distance, hardly trying to catch him. They knew there was no escape. The corridor was sealed tight. He'd never get away.

He leaned against a wall and glanced at the ring. It was no longer clear as crystal, but glowed bright orange. It had become hot enough to burn his finger. He'd have to take it off.

The creatures were twenty feet away.

He pulled on the ring, clenching his teeth as the red-hot stone burned his fingers. As he touched it, the stone pressed down. A hatch door slid open beside him, revealing the fresh, damp starry night of Earth he had thought he'd never see again.

The orange stone stopped burning and turned clear. He thought of his family's garage door opener with its red-light sensors. Maybe the ring was also a door opener of some sort.

He jumped from the ship into the black hole of night.

His fall seemed to take forever, as if he'd jumped from someplace high in midair. His eyes focused on familiar trees, bushes, and a quivering mass of black and white just below him.

He fell on a pile of brush and rolled, coming to a stop near Aggie's soft, furry belly.

The trembling cow let out a long, loud, complaining moo.

"Oh, Aggie, you're free! Our friend Josiah set you free!"

Mike sprang to his feet and hugged her once quickly, afraid he'd never get to hug her again if they didn't get out of there fast.

The ship swung gently above them, its bluish-red lights burning bright. Suddenly, they went out in a flash of white light and bad-smelling smoke.

Mike grabbed Aggie by the collar and pulled. She wouldn't budge. Her legs shook like jelly. He smacked her hard on the rump and she bolted. He'd never seen her run so fast. In seconds she was rounding the trail toward the pasture gate.

The damaged oval disk shivered, sputtered, and glowed against the round full moon beyond. Mike glanced up at it once and thought he saw Josiah waving from one of its small round windows. He waved back blindly and stared open-mouthed at the retreating disk.

A blue-white light shone in a ring of dots from the bottom of the craft. It shot sideways and then stopped. The blue-white light flickered out behind it and then glowed very brightly. It took off again like out of a slingshot, and made an arc into the sky, then went up at an angle and quickly disappeared.

He ran for home. At least he thought he was headed for home. It was hard to tell, as he pushed through scratchy bushes and leaped over fallen logs, if he was really heading home or just running in circles.

After an eternity of running blindly in darkness, he found Allison's flashlight. She must have gotten home. He flicked it on. Training its beam around him, he recognized the path he was on. It wasn't too far from home. Home!

He glanced up into the sky. Fiery red fingers reached over the treetops behind him. The rotating searchlights were back. The ship had taken off and was invisible now, but could very well be lurking somewhere high above the clouds.

Maybe it couldn't return to orbit, if it was too badly damaged in the crash, or maybe the Fabrians were going to hang around and get him when he came out of the woods.

No matter what, he was going home. *Now*.

He inhaled the strong smell of pine needles and damp earth, and wondered if Allison or his parents had called the police.

He tipped his head back and peered through the branches, hoping not to see that silvery oval shape high up in the sky. He drew a sharp breath. The ship moved out from behind a cloud and hovered right above him, ready to pounce.

They can't get me if I stay in the woods, he told himself. Fear choked him, making it hard to breathe. He could imagine a giant laser beam coming down from the ship and sucking him back up into it. Was it his imagination, or was the ship moving lower and closer?

The wide round moon moved behind a cloud and the ship went completely dark. A noise like thunder rumbled right over Mike's head. He stopped and stared at the empty sky, touching Josiah's ring on his finger.

Silently, he trudged along the trail as the moon moved out again, lighting his way. His shadow fell across the brush like a looming monster, but he didn't have the energy to be afraid anymore.

He walked on, his legs trembling with every step, up a small rise to the last tree before his grassy back yard. Then he groaned and sank onto one of Allison's swings.

The back door's only a few hundred feet away and I can't go any further, he thought.

He noticed a raccoon tipping over a garbage can, spilling its contents all over the patio. As if I haven't had enough problems, he grumbled to himself, now I'll be expected to clean up the mess in the morning. In fact, it probably *was* morning.

Suddenly he felt even more tired. He glanced up toward the bedroom windows at the back of the house. They were dark.

*Where is everybody?*

Didn't they see the fire in the sky? Didn't they hear the horses and cows complaining? The spaceship crashing through the treetops? Surely, Allison must have told them . . .

Beep . . . beep . . . beep . . .

*Told them what?*

Mike crawled through the darkened house to his room. Pushing himself to his last ounce of strength, he flopped down on his bed. He could hear soft snores coming from Allison's room.

Only the dog seemed to notice his return. As Mike lay limp across the covers, Herman licked his hand and sniffed Josiah's ring. Then he growled softly at it.

Turning his head toward the window, Mike gazed out at the starry sky and saw a bright light beside the moon.

Herman ran to the window, wagged his tail, and growled again.

"Go to sleep, dog, it's a shooting star," Mike muttered. Lifting his hand, he stared at the strange ring he wore. He rubbed it with his finger and held it to his nose. It smelled like pine needles and earth.

He tried to remember where it came from, and why it was fastened tightly above the knuckle on his finger. He never wore rings.

His clothes were damp, muddy, and he was exhausted, perspiring from head to toe. His watch said 1:00 A.M. Only fifteen minutes ago, he'd been yelling at Allison to get back in bed. She'd been at the window, watching a shooting star. . . .

# GHOST TWIN

## by Mark Valadez

# 1

Charlie came to me the summer before I started the seventh grade. I was brushing my teeth in the bathroom mirror, making sure to get the back teeth too, when my mirror image started talking to me.

"Hello, Peter!"

I froze, my candy-cane toothbrush—I know, I know, it's a silly stocking stuffer Grandma gave me last Christmas—dangling from my frothy lip. The freckle-face in the mirror started to laugh at me. "You look like a werewolf. Your mouth is all white and foamy."

I asked, "Who are you?", and instantly felt silly because it was *my* face in the mirror. Yet it wasn't.

"C'mon, Peter, don't be a dweeb. You know who I am. I'm your brother."

I swallowed my toothpaste. "Charlie?"

"Yeah!"

Mom and Dad had told me about Charlie. Charles Daniel Hastings III, named after my father and grandfather; my twin brother born a minute and thirty seconds before me. But Charlie was . . . *dead*. He'd died being born.

Mom and Dad waited until I was about seven to tell me about him, said they thought I should know. But I'd already heard Grandma whispering about "Charlie," talking about him like he was still alive: "Such a beautiful baby Charlie was . . . " Once she called *me* Charlie and Mom got kind of mad about it, and I couldn't understand why.

I asked her about it: "Mom, who's Charlie?"

She looked surprised and maybe a little scared. "What did you just say, Peter?"

"Who's this Charlie Grandma's always talking about?"

She changed the subject, but later that day

she and Dad sat me down and told me the story. They told me how Charlie was in heaven, that he was my guardian angel and he'd always watch over me.

Sure enough, since then there'd been times when I was sure I felt him with me. I couldn't quite explain it, but I knew I wasn't alone, and I sort of liked that. Like in the third grade when Billy Steens had said he was going to beat me up after school. I was really scared walking home. My palms were sweaty and my heart was pounding. I kept expecting Billy to jump out of every corner. He never showed though—I found out later he'd gone home early to have his tonsils out and cried about it, they told me, in the nurse's office.

Still, the whole time I was walking home, looking over my shoulder every couple of steps, I'd pretended Charlie was walking right alongside me, escorting me home like my own private bodyguard or something, telling me not to worry—"I'll take care of you, Peter."

Now here he was, and it wasn't me putting words in his mouth, imagining what he'd say if he were here. No. He really was here.

"Are you just going to stand there all day with

that stupid look on your face?"

He started to make funny faces at me in the mirror, imitating my gaping stare, crossing my . . . uh, excuse me, *his* eyes.

I was lucky I didn't hurt myself when I fell over.

It was a few weekends later, and I was sleeping over at my best friend Kevin Wellburn's house. His sister, Jennifer, was there with her friend Gina and the new kid from down the block, Thad, who'd more or less invited himself. We ordered pizza, played video games and watched some silly old dinosaur movie on *Friday Night Creature Features*.

Kev and Jennifer were twins, just like Charlie and I were. The only difference was, Kev was a boy, Jennifer was a girl. Kev and I shared a lot of secrets, but for some reason I'd never told him about Charlie. Not before, and certainly not about what had happened lately. But I was thinking about it. I was thinking hard.

"These dinosaurs don't even look real," Thad kept saying, not letting anyone watch the movie in peace.

"Oh, Thad, why don't you just watch the

movie, okay?"

Thad had moved into Chris Bell's old house over the summer. He was an only child, like me, but he didn't seem to have many friends, and he tried too hard to make them. He'd be real quiet for a stretch, then start up again, showing off for Jennifer, who he'd really seemed to try to latch on to. "That's supposed to be a Tyrannosaurus rex, you know."

"And that's a dufus clownus." Kev pointed at him and laughed.

"Real funny, Wellburn." Thad got all red in the face and started mumbling to himself.

The movie ended around nine o'clock, and somebody—I think it was Gina—had the bright idea to tell ghost stories. Gina scared me enough as it was. She was a whole foot taller than me, and her fastball was murder.

In any case, we shut off the lights in the basement and settled in. We sat in a circle on top of the pool table, our legs folded Indian-style. The refrigerator was humming in the corner, and the room was bathed in a weird blue light from Kev's fish tank, which was also humming.

Jennifer went first, holding a flashlight under her chin to make herself look spooky. What was really spooky about it was how much she looked like Kev. Same dimples, same curly brown hair. It was weird. I'd never thought about it much before. This whole twin thing was getting to me.

"Okay," Jennifer said. "Here we go . . ."

"This isn't going to be about some guy with a hook, is it?" Kev asked.

"No. Now hush and listen . . . this is a true story. It really happened to Allison Bauer's older sister in college. She was living in a dorm with this other girl. And one night she was out late studying at the library because she had a big test the next day."

"What kind of test?" Kev wanted to know.

"I don't know . . . math test or something. Look, it doesn't really matter, okay? What happened was—it was really late at night, and she was really scared walking back to the dorm because there was an escaped maniac on the loose . . ."

"Oh, one of *those* guys again," I chimed in.

"Are you going to let me tell the story?"

"Sorry, go on," I said.

Jennifer took the flashlight from her face and sighed. "See? You made me forget where I was now."

"There was an escaped maniac on the loose,"

Thad said, looking pleased with himself.

"That's right, Thad, there was."

I thought Thad was going to faint and fall off the pool table when Jennifer said that to him.

Jennifer took a deep breath and continued. "So she gets home and she lets herself into her room, right? But she doesn't turn on the lights, because she doesn't want to wake up her roommate. It's dark and there's just a little bit of moonlight coming through the window, enough to see her roommate curled up in bed on her side, fast asleep..."

I stole a glance at Gina. She was pinching her palm and biting down on her knuckle. Thad's eyes were as wide as saucers, and he kept adjusting his glasses which would slide down his nose like clockwork every two minutes. You could set your watch by it. Kev was picking at a worn patch of felt on top of the pool table, but his eyes never left Jennifer.

"...She tiptoed through the room as quietly as she could, putting away her stuff and finding her pajamas in the dark. She was just getting into bed when she heard it...a rustling sound coming from the other side of the room. 'Lisa,' she whispered. That was her roommate's name.

'Lisa' . . . no answer.

"She didn't think much of it. She figured it was just Lisa tossing in her sleep. But then she heard it again. She wanted to turn on the lights. Just for a second to make sure everything was okay. But she knew Lisa would be mad if she woke her up. Lisa was a real light sleeper.

"So she lay there in bed, the covers pulled up to her chin. She listened again for the noise, but there was nothing. Just the sound of crickets chirping outside the window.

"She was drifting off to sleep when . . . there it was again. A rustling. It sounded like it was coming from underneath Lisa's bed."

"Maybe it was a mouse," Kev snickered.

"Come on, you guys," Gina whined. "I want to hear this."

Jennifer went on. "She wanted to put on the lights, but she was afraid . . . afraid of what she might find. So she just lay there. Listening. Waiting. Afraid to breathe. Finally, somehow, some way, she fell asleep . . ."

"S-So what happened?" Thad asked in a shaky voice.

"She woke up the next morning with the sun streaming through the window. She was all sleepy and she'd forgotten how scared she'd been the night before. It was daylight now and every-thing was fine . . . or so she *thought*."

Just then the headlights of a passing car washed over us through one of the tiny basement level windows, and everyone's heart skipped a beat. At least mine did.

"Come on, Jen!" Gina demanded, "What on earth happened?"

Jennifer shuddered and went on. "She rolled over in bed and stared across the room. It took a couple of seconds for her eyes to focus. Then she saw it." Jennifer suddenly raised her voice, shouting. "There!"

Without warning, the lights flew on. Gina screamed and pointed at the cork bulletin board across the room. On it was scrawled in big red letters: "Aren't You Glad You Didn't Turn On The Lights?!"

# 2

The scream rattled my bones, and this time Thad *did* fall off the pool table. It was then that I realized it wasn't Gina screaming . . . it was

Thad. What a goof!

Gina had already made a beeline for the stairs, but stopped at the landing when she heard Jennifer laughing. I looked over and saw Kev standing between the pool table and the light switch. He walked calmly toward the cork bulletin board, touched a finger to the scrawled message and tested it. "Lipstick," he said, grinning slyly.

Jennifer was holding her side she was laughing so hard. "Is that not the best?" she choked out at us.

Thad's head popped up over the edge of the pool table, his glasses hanging lopsided off his face.

"We'd been planning that one all day," Kev announced. "Scared you guys good, didn't we?"

Just then the door swung open at the top of the stairs. Kev and Jennifer's mom stood there, peering down at us. "*What* is going on down here?"

Jennifer's eyes widened and she made an "uh-oh" face. "It's okay, Mom, we're just playing."

Mrs. Wellburn put her arm around Gina and led her back down the stairs. "Gina, you're shaking all over."

"I'm okay," Gina muttered into her chest and threw a dirty look at Jennifer. "It wasn't *that* scary."

Thad was fumbling around on the other side of the room, bumping into things. Mrs. Wellburn took one look at him and said, "Thad, you're a nervous wreck."

"We were just telling spooky stories is all," Kev said, hurriedly wiping the lipstick message from the bulletin board.

"Well, take it easy on the spooky stories," Mrs. Wellburn said firmly, her hands on her hips. "You kids are going to scare each other so bad you won't sleep tonight. You'll turn each other's hair white."

Jennifer mouthed her mother's words as she said them and we all had to laugh. It was a favorite expression of Mrs. Wellburn's, like, "Kevin, you turn off those horror films this instant! You'll scare yourself so bad you'll turn your hair white!"

"Great, Mom," Kev would say. "Then I *really* will look like Grandad."

Mrs. Wellburn went back upstairs and everyone seemed to relax again. I suggested we play some more video games, but Gina seemed determined not to be upstaged by Jennifer. "I've got one," she said. "I've got a story."

"I'm with Peter," Thad said, his voice cracking. "I'm tired of listening to ghost stories."

"What's the matter, Thad? Are you *scared*?" Gina mimicked an evil, rumbled laugh.

"N-No. I'm not scared. I'm just bored with it already."

"*Sure*! You're shaking in your shoes." Gina could be mean sometimes. I was starting to feel sorry for Thad.

"Come on, Gina," I said. "No one wants to hear your dumb story."

"It's not really a story. It's more like an experiment. You guys ever hear of May Worth?"

Kev said, "May who?"

Jennifer rolled her eyes and groaned knowingly. "Oh, you mean that silly thing with the mirror?"

Did someone say "mirror"? I don't look at mirrors anymore. I already know what I look like. Do I hear my mother calling me? Can I cut out now?

But there we were again, sitting around in a circle on top of the pool table, the lights dimmed. We listened as Gina explained. May Worth was a woman who lived about a hundred years ago, when the neighborhood was filled with spooky old Victorian mansions, and buggies and horse-drawn carriages still roamed the streets. She practiced witchcraft, died, and was said to still haunt the area.

I was wondering what Mr. and Mrs. Wellburn were watching on TV upstairs. Maybe they'd like some company.

Gina was saying, "If you look into a mirror and say 'I believe in May Worth' three times, you'll see her reflection."

"Get out of here," Kev scoffed.

"No, it's for real," she insisted. "Karen Nash, this girl in our class, tried it. It works."

Slowly, as if on the same wavelength, we all turned our heads at the same time, eyeing the bathroom door in the corner.

Jennifer said, "I'll give a dollar to whoever tries it."

We all looked at each other. It was put-up or shut-up time. Thad was breathing heavily beside me. I knew he had asthma, and I worried that if we kept on with this, he'd have an attack before the night was out. Maybe I would too.

"What's the matter?" Gina asked. "No takers? Not one?"

"Why don't *you* do it?" I threw the ball back in her court. "You're the one who brought it up."

"We'll all do it," Kev said. "But we'll draw straws to see who goes first. Jen, go upstairs and get some toothpicks."

"I'm not your slave. You go get them."

"I'm older."

"Oh gee whiz . . . by all of twenty seconds too." Who could argue with that?

Kev trudged up the stairs and returned a few minutes later with a handful of old Number 2 pencils. "I couldn't find any toothpicks," he said, "and Mom wouldn't let me use any of those wooden kitchen matches, so I thought we'd use these. The erasers are all worn down anyway."

Gina grabbed a pencil, took one look at the chewed-up eraser and grimaced. "Yuck! Get hungry much, Kev?"

We broke up the pencils, placed them all inside an old cardboard school box and shook it up. Jennifer passed the box around and we all had to reach in without looking and pick. We decided to go in pairs—safety in numbers—and whoever got the two shortest pieces had to go first.

Guess who?

Thad and I stood side by side in front of the bathroom mirror. The door was closed and we could hear them outside, whispering among themselves.

"This is stupid," I said loud enough for them to hear. "How long are we supposed to stand here?"

"Until you see May Worth," Kev called back.

"How will we recognize her? I don't even know what she looked like."

I was playing the clown, trying to conceal my fear. The thing was—it wasn't May Whatshername I was worried about.

"Are you okay, Thad?" I could hear his teeth chattering in the dark.

"I'm not going to look, I'm not going to look..." He repeated it over and over again in a hoarse whisper, trembling next to me.

"Oh yeah," I cried. "There she is, I see her. Boy, is that scary! Can we come out now?"

"We've to hear you say the words," Kev shouted back. "She won't come unless you say it."

I wanted it to be over and done with, so I took a deep breath and said it. Fast. Three times. "I believe in May Worth...I believe in May Worth...I believe in May Worth..."

I stared into the mirror and held my breath. Waiting. Nothing. Only two faces. Mine and . . . well, the top of Thad's head anyway. He had his head down, chin tucked into his chest, eyes squeezed shut. Everything was dead still, only the sound of the faucet dripping steadily.

"Do you see her?" he whispered. "Do you see her?"

My reflection smiled back at me. "You can open your eyes now, Thad. If she was ever there, she's gone now."

So much for May Worth.

That night, the girls slept upstairs in Jennifer's room, while we guys camped out in our sleeping bags in the basement. Everything had calmed down. Even Thad's nerves seemed to have recovered. He slept like a log while Kev snored like a sea lion.

I was wide awake, staring at Kev's saltwater tropicals as they swam around inside the fish tank. My throat was dry, so I got up and headed into the bathroom for a drink of water. I stood at the faucet, filling a paper cup.

"Hello, Peter."

I dropped the cup into the sink and splashed

water all over the front of my pajamas. Charlie smiled at me from inside the mirror, raising his hand and wiggling his fingers. "So who's this May Worth?"

Just as quickly as he appeared that night, he disappeared. But it wasn't long before I saw Charlie again.

I went home the next morning. I stared in the mirror for hours and hours, speaking to my reflection. "Come back, Charlie. Come back. I'm not afraid anymore. I want to talk. There's so many things I want to ask you." But he wouldn't show himself.

Mom came in and asked if I was feeling all right.

"You don't have a fever," she said, feeling my forehead with the flat of her hand.

"I'm okay," I said. "Can I ask you something though?"

"Sure."

"It's about Charlie."

Her forehead wrinkled with concern and she

sat down on the edge of my bed. "Yes, Peter?"

"Are you sure . . . ?"

She waited. "Sure about what?"

"Nothing. It's stupid."

She sighed and put her arm around my shoulder, pulling me close. "What's bothering you, Peter? Tell me."

I didn't know what to say to her. "I guess it's just . . . I think about him a lot lately."

"I think about him a lot too. Every day of my life."

She leaned in close to me and pointed her chin at the window. "Look out there. You see that sunset?"

I followed her eyes out into the backyard. The weather vane and bird feeder on top of our shed were capped in a soft purplish-red haze—what Mrs. Clark, the sixth-grade art teacher, liked to call magenta. I must have seen it a thousand times, but I never really paid much attention.

"Look how beautiful," Mom said. "If you look carefully, you'll see every color of the spectrum. It takes your breath away. Then it's gone."

I gave her a look. "It happens every night, Mom."

"My point is, Peter, that's the nature of all

things beautiful. They last a short time, then they're gone, like Charlie."

I turned and looked again at the sunset. It was sinking fast, blotted out by the shed, the fence; darkness was falling. Then it was gone.

School started up again the following Monday. Jennifer took the bus with Gina, Thad, and just about every other kid on our block who went to middle school. But Kev and I had to be different. We were in the seventh grade now, and we were going to ride our bikes like a lot of the eighth-graders did. We'd gone on a trial run over the summer, scouting out the best possible shortcut past the railroad tracks, and no amount of good sense could talk us out of it.

I got ready in the morning, had breakfast and checked in the mirror for Charlie. It was getting to be a habit. Then I was off, telling Mom good-bye on the way out the door and heading down the block for the bus stop at the corner of Rhodes Court. Once I was sure Mom was no longer watching from the window, I doubled back, care-fully walking my bike out of the garage and winging over to the next block.

Kev was waiting for me at the entrance to

Fletcher Park, riding around in circles and popping wheelies by the basketball hoops. He beamed when he saw me. "I didn't think you were going to show. I thought for sure they'd *carry* you onto that bus."

"I suppose you're such a big man, your mom and dad didn't give you any argument."

"I knew what they would say, so I didn't even bother to ask."

I had a bad thought. "Jennifer's going to squeal on you. I bet you any amount."

"She better not. She knows who the boss is."

If she'd have been there, she would have popped him one. I've seen it happen.

"We better go," I said. "We'll be late if we don't get a move on."

We heard him before we saw him. "Hey, you kids?"

I froze. My heart jumped, and I went weak in the chest. I knew the feeling well from the Billy Steens era.

"You kids get out of there! Now!"

It was Bubble-Eye, the park custodian. We called him that because one of his eyes was bigger than the other, and it bulged like in a cartoon whenever he was angry. I'd hardly ever seen him any other way. He'd come barreling out of his shanty office like a fire-breathing monster, chasing after older kids who were messing around on the slides and swings—there was a sign that said you couldn't go on those things if you were over twelve. Otherwise, he was running off kids for riding bikes on the basketball courts. That was another sign—along with no spitting, no foul language, and no letting your dog drink out of the water fountains.

Bubble-Eye was heading right for us, waving that big stick he used to spear and pick up pieces of trash. "Can't you kids read? Get those bikes out of there!"

Kev pedaled the blacktop a couple of times, giving himself a running start. He was scared. So was I. I couldn't get my bike turned around fast enough. We were out of there like a shot, Bubble-Eye standing under the hoops, shaking his stick at us from behind the chain-link fence.

It was just that kind of morning.

"That was close," Kev was saying. "If he'd have caught you, he would have swiped us with that stick." Kev cracked himself up with that one.

"Yeah, right."

"You know, he has kids' scalps hanging on the wall inside that office."

"Kev, that's gross!"

Kev was laughing. "He can put a curse on you with that eye too. It's the evil eye."

I gave Kev a look. "It's not funny really. Remember Coach Simon from Little League?"

"Yeah?"

"Well, he caught Sean Miller making fun of Bubble-Eye this one time. You know how Sean used to be able to close one eye and imitate him?"

"Yeah, that was the best."

"Well, Coach Simon didn't think it was very funny. He told us Bubble-Eye has something wrong with him, and that's why his eye's like that."

"For real?"

"For real. I don't laugh at him anymore for that reason."

There were two sets of railroad tracks running side by side in each direction. They stretched for miles through Hollister Tunnel. Kev was riding on one side and I was riding on the other.

"What if two trains were coming," Kev said. "One coming this way and one from behind.

What would you do?"

"I'd get out of the way, you goof!"

"But what if you didn't have time?"

I thought about it and shuddered. "I guess I'd get between the two tracks."

Kev shook his head and rolled his eyes. "Hastings, what would you do without me? You'd be dead if you did that. You'd get run over for sure. My Uncle Steve works for the railroad, and he told me that the train would pull you right under. The force is too great."

I saw Hollister Tunnel looming large ahead of us like a gaping mouth waiting to devour . . . either that or it would burp up a train. I suddenly had a very bad feeling about this shortcut.

I turned on Kev. "Well, this was *real* smart then!"

"Relax," he said. "I told you. My Uncle Steve works for the railroad. I got the schedule down cold. Trains don't run in the morning on Mondays, Wednesdays and Fridays. Which means we'd best go the long way around tomorrow."

"Are you sure?"

"Positive. I think."

"*What?*"

"I'm *kidding!* Relax."

We were silent for a bit. Then I asked him, "Kev, what's it like being a twin?"

"Huh?"

"You heard me."

Kev looked at me like I'd asked him what planet we were on. "It's not like anything really. I don't even think Jen and I look that much alike. See, we're fraternal twins, not identical. We look a little bit alike because we're brother and sister, but we don't look exactly alike. We were just born at the same time. That's what fraternal means. Why?"

I shrugged. "Just curious."

He looked at me and shook his head. "You've sure been acting funny lately, Peter."

I didn't know what to say to him. Should I tell him about Charlie? I hadn't seen him for a while. Maybe he was gone. I decided to let it go.

"C'mon," I said as we came up on the tunnel. "I'll race you to the end."

"You're on!"

We pumped our legs and picked up speed, sailing headlong into the blackness, the wind in our faces. The tunnel stretched a good two hundred yards over Willow Creek where Grandpa used to take me ice fishing in the winters. When he'd died, Grandma said he'd gone on to a better place. I wondered if Charlie was there too.

I was lost in these and other thoughts when the ground started to vibrate. At first I didn't think much of it. Then the tunnel started to shake. I heard Kev screaming: "Train! Oh my gosh! Peter, it's a train!"

# 4

I felt the start in my chest at the same time I heard the whistle, shrill and piercing, a distant whine at first, growing louder. I turned to look over my shoulder and saw the mouth of the tunnel close up, then a beacon of light growing out of the darkness.

"Speed up," Kev shouted. "Speed up!"

We were little more than halfway though the tunnel, and the opening at the end, at first a tiny circle of light, had grown wider, blue sky and prairie visible beyond. I pumped my legs, felt them aching as I aimed headlong for the exit, screaming.

I felt something catch in the spokes of my wheel, no, my pedal, slowing me down. Something was pulling to me to my right—...*the train will pull you right under. The force is too great.*

I panicked and toppled over on my side, falling against the wall of the tunnel. I realized then my shoelace was tangled up on my right pedal. I was trapped, a goner. The train was bearing down and would pull me right under when it passed. I started to scream.

Kev had already cleared the tunnel. I heard him shouting my name. "Pete! Pete! Where are you?"

I could hear the train getting closer, felt the heat, smelled it. Then I felt a tug on my foot. Charlie was squatting beside me, holding my shoe. *Charlie.*

"Run," he screamed. "Run!"

I rose up and tore out of there, the sunlight hitting me full in the face. I heard the whistle at my back, blaring, deafening, a horrible squealing and twisting of metal that could only have been my bike. I fell to the right, dropping and rolling in the tall grass. About twenty seconds later, the train roared past, rumbling and belching like some ferocious creature.

I stood up, drenched with sweat, tears rolling

down my face. As the train moved past, I could glimpse between the gaps in the cars, Kev was standing on the other side. The caboose cleared, and there he was about fifty feet away.

"Pete! You're alive!" he shouted. He was crying too.

I hobbled around in a daze. I was only wearing one shoe.

A few days later, I checked carefully in the mirror. Not for Charlie, but to see if my hair was turning white. It had not. At least not yet anyway. I was sure the train incident would have done it, if anything would.

Needless to say, Mom and Dad were very upset. And here I was the one who'd lost my bike, my new backpack too. It wasn't a pretty scene. "I'll take you by the hand and *walk* you to that bus stop if I have to," Dad said.

Of course, Mr. and Mrs. Wellburn heard all about it and took Kev's bike away from him. Jennifer told everyone Kev would be old enough to drive a car before he got it back. Kev said if he played his cards right, maybe by fourteen.

I was shook up for about a week. What a way to kick off the new school year! Everyone in class had heard about it. In about a hundred different versions too, none of which even came close to what really happened. Even the most outlandish rumors couldn't compete with what *I* knew—the ghost of my twin brother had saved my life. I guess Mom and Dad were right. Charlie *was* my guardian angel.

It was about a week before Halloween. I was sitting with Kev and Jennifer in the school cafeteria. It was just the three of us at our table. Gina had a different lunch period, and Thad had been out all week with the chicken pox.

Kev was playing with his dessert. "What *is* this stuff?"

"Tapioca pudding."

"I hate it."

Jennifer glared at him and looked for all the world like their mother. "Why didn't you get the Jell-O then?"

"Because Timmy Campbell took the last one, that's why." Kev put down his spoon in disgust.

"Speak of the devil," I said.

Timmy Campbell walked by, shaking up his chocolate milk. He looked at me and started making train noises, cocking his elbow and pumping his arm like a train conductor. "Choo-Choooo!"

I shook my head and rolled my eyes. "Am I supposed to laugh now or later?"

*He* must have thought it was funny because he walked off laughing. Then again, this was the guy who thought huge sopping wads of wet toilet paper stuck to the walls of the boys' room was an absolute scream.

Jennifer got real quiet all of sudden. Then she said, "If I tell you guys something, you promise not to laugh?"

Kev arched an eyebrow. "Depends on what it is."

Jennifer narrowed her eyes and hissed. "Just forget it," she said.

Kev's curiosity got the better of him. "No, I'm sorry, Jen, please! I want to know, tell me!"

She pushed her chair in closer to the table and leaned forward on her elbows, speaking in hushed tones. "Well, remember that day when you guys almost got hit by the train?"

Kev and I looked at each other. "Unfortunately, yes."

Jennifer fidgeted uncomfortably, cracking her knuckles. "Well, I was on the bus with Gina, and . . ."

Kev bobbed his head with impatient anticipation. "Uh-huh? . . . Yeah? Any time now."

"Well, I just . . . I got this feeling of horror, you know?"

"What do you mean?"

"Like I knew something bad was happening, but I wasn't sure what."

Emily Willis dropped her tray about twenty feet away. The loud clattering of plastic dishes made us all jump. Timmy Campbell led his table in applause, and it spread like Thad's chicken pox through the lunchroom. Mr. Thomas, the gym teacher/lunch monitor blew his whistle—he kept it on a chain around his neck—and everyone quieted down, but only after our nerves had been pretty well frayed.

Kev wrinkled his nose at Jennifer. "Jen, you're starting to sound like Aunt Wanda now."

I'd heard Kev and Jennifer talking about their Aunt Wanda. She lived in an old house in nearby Liberty Oaks, wore jewelry like a gypsy, and read tarot cards and told people's fortunes at the county fairs. There was one coming up that weekend.

"I'm serious," Jennifer was saying. "I don't

know how to explain, but it was there. And it's still there."

Kev gave up on the tapioca pudding and pushed away his tray. "Maybe you should ask her. Aunt Wanda, I mean."

"Will you guys come with me?" She looked at us with pleading eyes. I'd rarely seen her this way.

"Why don't you ask Gina to go with you?"

"She can't. She's going away with her family this weekend. What do you say, guys?"

Kev and I exchanged frowns. "Sure."

The bell rang, and we gathered up our stuff to go back to class. I wondered if Aunt Wanda would know about Charlie. And if she did, would *I* want to know?

I was sitting in sixth-period Social Studies class listening to Mrs. Hamill drone on about the Boston Tea Party. Timmy Campbell had his head down on his desk two rows over, drooling a small river onto his spiral notebook. The last thing in the world I expected to see was Charlie peeking in behind the glass door pane at the back of the room.

He was making faces at me, sticking his

tongue out and crossing his eyes. He squished his nose up against the door pane, but—a curious thing—he didn't fog up the glass. Then he did the creepiest thing; he bent his neck to the side and held an invisible rope above his head like he was hanging from a noose, his eyes bugged out, his tongue hanging.

I felt my blood run cold inside my veins, and the back of my neck prickled like an electrical current all the way down to the small of my back. My textbook slid off the edge of my desk and landed with a loud, resounding Thwap! An explosion like Timmy Campbell made when he stomped on milk cartons in the cafeteria.

Everyone turned with a start to look at me. Timmy Campbell fell out of his desk babbling: "I'm up, Ma! I'm up!"

Mrs. Hamill glared at me from the front of the room.

She said, "Is there a problem, Mr. Hastings?"

I felt thirty pairs of eyes boring into me. "Uh, could I be excused to use the lavatory, please?" We couldn't just say "bathroom", we had to say lavatory. Mrs. Hamill's class, her rules.

She took her glasses off and sighed. "Right in the middle of the Boston Tea Party. Why not? Go ahead, but make it quick."

I hurried up to her desk and she handed me a hall pass. Timmy Campbell, fully awake now, was raising his hand. "I've got to go too."

"Wait until Peter gets back. Now, where were we?"

I stepped out into the hall, closing the door behind me. I nearly gave myself whiplash scanning the halls for Charlie. It was no use, he was gone.

"Pssst! Pete, over here."

I spun around in time to see a head of dark blonde hair peeking around the corner at the far end of the hall. I heard him giggle as he hightailed it back the other way. *Charlie*! He was here!

# 5

The halls were empty. It was just him and me.

I sprinted after him, sliding on my sneakers as I rounded the corner. He stopped, let me gain a few feet, then turned and fled, giggling as he ducked into the boys' room.

I dove in after him, determined not to let him get away. I cursed when I found the bathroom empty. I checked the stalls, the *mirror*!...Nothing. He had done it to me again.

"Boo!"

I jumped two feet, spinning on my heel.

"Hello, Peter."

He was standing right in front of me. Smiling, dangling a yo-yo from his right hand. He sure looked real. He wasn't pale or anything, or transparent, like you see in cartoons or comic books. He seemed to be made of flesh and blood, and he was wearing *my* clothes. It was like...well, looking in a mirror.

He said, "Are you just going to stand there all day with that stupid look on your face?"

"Ch-Charlie?"

"Naw, it's May Worth!" He started giggling again. "You sure do have some kooky friends."

"What are you doing here?"

He kept his eyes fixed on the yo-yo. "I came to see *you*."

"But why?"

He met my eyes. "It's a good thing for you I was around that day by the railroad tracks."

I shuddered thinking about it. "Yeah, well, thanks...I guess."

He mimicked me. "Thanks, I guess..."

My eyes were drawn to the yo-yo. It was bright red with a wacky design on the front. It wasn't like any I'd ever seen. "Where'd you get the yo-yo?"

"It's Grandpa's." He said it like it was the most natural thing in the world.

"Grandpa gave you a yo-yo?" It's crazy, I know, but I was a little jealous.

"It belonged to him when he was a little boy. They don't make them like this anymore. It's from the thirties, forties... something like that. It's a vintage Forrester."

He started doing tricks with it, rolling it up his arm, over his shoulder, behind his back. "This one's called walking the dog," he said.

"Did *Grandpa* teach you those tricks?"

"Uh-huh."

"Talk to Grandpa a lot, I suppose?"

"Now and then."

I wasn't feeling so good. "Why are you here, Charlie?"

He made a face like he was losing patience with me. "I told you. I came to see *you*." He offered the yo-yo in an outstretched hand. "Here, you try it."

I touched his fingers as I accepted the yo-yo.

They were ice-cold.

"Go ahead," he said. "Give it a shot. It's easy once you get the hang of it."

I tried to do the "walking the dog" bit, but the string just got tangled up on my wrist.

"You stink!" He laughed, snatching the yo-yo back and showing me how it's done.

I thought it, and out it came. "Show-off!"

"You're just mad because you can't do it."

"I could if you teach me."

He clucked his tongue and wrinkled his brow like he was in deep thought. "What's in it for me?"

"What do you mean?"

"What I said. What's in it for me?"

"W-Well, what do you want?"

He thought about it for a second, then blurted, "Your catcher's mitt!"

"My catcher's mitt? What are *you* going to do with it?"

"What do you think?"

"But you're . . . *dead!*"

His smile curdled. A sad, hurt look filled his eyes.

"I'm sorry," was all I could think of to say.

The seventh-period bell rang and Mr. Hardy, the hall monitor, came in, his keyring jangling on his belt. "I *thought* I heard somebody in here. Peter, do you have a hall pass?"

I turned back to look at Charlie, but he was gone. I swallowed hard, staring down at the spot where he'd been standing.

"Peter?"

I turned back to Mr. Hardy. "Huh? What?"

He gave me a stern look, hands on his hips. "Do you have a hall pass?"

I held it up. He nodded and winked at me. He was an okay guy, Mr. Hardy. He turned back toward the door, then stopped.

"Are you okay, Peter?" he asked.

"Uh . . . yeah, sure. Why?"

"Well, you look like you've seen a ghost."

That Friday night, I went with Kev and Jennifer to the Liberty Oaks County Fair. My mom dropped us off around five. We arranged to meet her in an hour and a half, after promising to stick together as a group.

The fairgrounds were crowded and still a little damp from the previous night's rain. A lot of people, high school kids mainly, were walking around in costumes, getting a jump on Halloween Sunday night. We counted two grim reapers, four vampires, a handful of ghosts and one gumball machine. None of the ghosts looked like Charlie.

We saw a bunch of kids we knew from school, Bubble-Eye driving around in a Parks Department vehicle, and the kicker—Miss Davenport from third-period English standing in line to board the Ferris wheel with her fiancé. Kev thought it was the most amazing thing. He didn't think teachers had lives outside the classroom.

"Let's hit the Tilt-a-Whirl," he suggested.

Jennifer vetoed it. "The line's too long, and I want to see Aunt Wanda first." She was the one holding the money, so that completely ended that discussion.

Aunt Wanda had set up show in a little tent near the funhouse and bumper cars. She was a heavy lady who wore a lot of gold chains and medallions, and her streaky gray hair was tied up in a bun on top of her head. She spoke softly and seemed to be very friendly, offering us seats around a small card table topped with a black velvet cloth.

"Hey, Aunt Wanda," Kev said. "Jen wants to know about the man she's going to marry!"

Jennifer smacked him a good one in the shoulder, and Kev just about fell out of his chair.

"Easy now, kids," Aunt Wanda scolded them in a firm but easy voice. "Play nice."

Jennifer apologized. "Sorry, Aunt Wanda. He's just a pain sometimes."

Aunt Wanda addressed them with the most hypnotic blue eyes I'd ever seen. "Yes, but you love him."

Jennifer made a face. "I wouldn't go *that* far."

Aunt Wanda smile knowingly. "Sure you do."

Jennifer went on to explain the feeling of horror that overcame her the day Kev and I were nearly hit by the train.

"Twins have a very strong bond," Aunt Wanda said. "I once knew a woman who felt a sudden, sharp pain in her arm for no reason. She found out later that her brother—her twin—had injured his arm in a skiing accident in another state at virtually the same instant. Psychic bonds between twins are quite common."

Kev suddenly became very serious, remembering. "I never told anybody, but once, in the second grade, I started itching for no reason. Jen was away at camp, but she came home early because she had caught..."

"Poison ivy." Jennifer finished the sentence.

Aunt Wanda saw we were all a little spooked and tried to lighten things. She blew on her fingernails. "I told you I'm good. Really though, it's nothing to be afraid of. Twins are supposed to be close."

I just sat there listening, not saying anything, but I noticed Aunt Wanda kept staring at me. It made me nervous. I felt as though she saw right through me. I couldn't wait to get out of there.

Kev and Jennifer chatted with Aunt Wanda for a few more minutes about their family, things in general. Finally, they said their good-byes and we headed out to leave and enjoy the carnival. I had one foot outside the tent when Aunt Wanda froze me with her words: "Kids, why don't you wait outside? I'd like to talk to Peter alone for a minute."

It hit me then. Charlie! She knew about Charlie!

I sat down again facing Aunt Wanda at the card table. She fixed me with an unblinking stare as she absently shuffled and reshuffled a deck of tarot cards.

"I didn't mean to alarm you," she said. "But I could sense something troubling you. And I could sense you felt uncomfortable talking about it in front of Kevin and Jennifer."

I hunched my shoulders, shivering slightly against the dampness, and took a breath. "I guess I'm still shook up from what happened with the train."

She shook her head. "No, it's more than that. Don't be afraid, Peter. You're among friends."

She said "friends" with an "s", meaning more than one, and I don't think she meant Kev and Jennifer, who were standing around outside devouring cotton candy. I looked around the tent, fearful of what "friends" she meant.

She fingered her beads and said, "You're a twin too, aren't you?"

I swallowed hard and nodded. "I have a brother. His name is Charlie."

"*Is* . . . not was?"

She was the real goods, it seemed. Kev and Jennifer didn't know about Charlie . . . not yet. There was no way Aunt Wanda could have known.

"Yes, he's been showing up lately, but no one else can see him."

She closed her eyes and took my hand. It was soft and warm to the touch, not icy like Charlie's. "I can see him," she said.

"I don't know whether to be afraid or not," I told her. "He saved my life, but . . . well, this stuff just isn't normal."

She opened her eyes. "Sometimes when a soul is not at rest, he or she hangs on."

"Should I be afraid?" I asked.

She closed her eyes again and squeezed my hand. Tighter. "You must be careful. He wants something he can't have."

"What?"

". . . to be you."

I walked out of there in a daze. Kev and Jennifer were on me in seconds. "What happened? What'd she tell you?"

"Nothing." I looked at the ground and kicked a soda can at my feet.

"Don't give me that," Kev said. "What'd she say?"

"Was it about Kev and me?" Jennifer wanted to know.

"No," I said. "It was about..."

I froze when I saw him. *Charlie!* He was standing in front of the Haunted House about a hundred feet away. He looked different, he looked scared... he was crying.

"Charlie!" I yelled, and watched him scamper away like a scared rabbit, disappearing into the Haunted House.

"Charlie?" Kev asked. "Who's Charlie?"

I ignored him and took off after my dead brother. I bypassed the line of kids waiting at the side entrance and hopped the gate. The attendant was shouting after me, red-faced. "Hey, you need a ticket!"

Kev and Jennifer chased after me, following my lead and ignoring the ticket taker. The other kids in line saw that, thought it was open season, and charged the gate. The attendant threw up his arms like, "I give up!" and was swamped by some two dozen grade-schoolers making a beeline for the Haunted House.

It was like a maze inside. The halls were dark

and narrow, twisting and lined with fun-house mirrors. Cobwebs hung from the ceiling and a headless piano player pounded on an old organ with skeleton hands hung from wires. Spooky music poured out of a pair of hanging speakers, filling the house to the rafters, and a hidden projector shone wispy white ghosts onto the walls.

I fought my way through the cobwebs and climbed a rickety flight of stairs to the second level, tripping a wire. A standing coffin popped open on cue and a mechanical Count Dracula bounded out to meet me. The Count's arms were crossed over his chest and his eyes lit up, blinking yellow. I pushed him back into his coffin and sprinted down the hall. "Charlie! Charlie, where are you?"

The place was filled with at least thirty screaming kids, running through the halls, climbing the bannisters. I could hear Kev and Jennifer calling my name. "Peter! Pete, where are you? Pete!"

I battled my way through the throng of bodies, all pushing and pulling for space, and found myself face to face with my reflection in the fun-house mirrors. I saw a dozen other laughing faces, all distorted. Fat kids became skinny, skinny kids became fat, and there I was, pale and ghostly, my eyes staring up with a dull glaze. I was . . . *dead*!

# 7

I screamed and jumped back. The floor opened up. A trapdoor! I was falling, hurtling through the darkness. A raspy evil laugh echoed through the void: BEWARE! . . . HE WHO ENTERS THE HOUSE OF . . . TCCHH . . . BEWARE! . . . HE WHO ENTERS THE HOUSE OF . . . TCCHH . . . BEWARE! . . .

A stupid broken record!

I landed at the foot of the slide. Splash! Right into a mud puddle.

"Hey!"

A lumpy shadow dwarfed me, a beefy hand took hold of my windbreaker and yanked me to my feet. It was Bubble-Eye, and he didn't look pleased.

"You little troublemaker! Sneaking into the Haunted House without paying! Where's your mom and dad?"

I gave him a tired look. Right now, Bubble-Eye was the least of my problems.

Sunday night. Halloween.

Kev was dressed as a cowboy, Jennifer as a witch. Me? I could have saved some money and gone in my own clothes. If anyone asked, I could have told them I was going trick-or-treating as Charlie. "Who's Charlie?" they would ask. "My ghost twin," I would say. But people were starting to think I was nuts as it was. So I settled for your plain old clown; plastic red nose, white face and the whole bit.

We met late that afternoon at Kev and Jennifer's house. We hit all the houses on our block and worked our way over to Platt Street. The last thing I wanted to talk about was what had happened Friday night at the fair, so I kept trying to distract them. I kept asking questions, the answers for which I really wasn't interested in.

"Thad still have the chicken pox?"

"He's getting over it, but he's still contagious. I talked to him last night on the phone and I told him he should just go as a kid with chicken pox. It would save him money on a costume," said Jennifer.

"What about Gina?"

"She's still visiting her cousins in the country. She's going trick-or-treating with them."

Three houses into Jones Street, we met up with Timmy Campbell and his brothers. Timmy was wearing his Little League uniform—Number 27—and said he was supposed to be a major league ballplayer. "I'm with the Red Sox," he announced proudly.

"Hate to burst your bubble there, Tim," Jennifer said. "But those aren't Red Sox colors."

He didn't know what to say to that. She had him there, so he turned on *me*. "I'm striking you out next Saturday, Hastings! You're done for!"

Jennifer leaped to my defense. "Oh, keep sucking on that sucker, sucker!"

Timmy's jaw dropped open and his grape sucker fell out of his mouth. Even his brothers had to crack up.

We kept on moving, heading down the block. We made it to old Mrs. Dunbar's house at the end. She was the one with the scarecrow on her front porch screen and Mama-Papa-Baby jack-o'-lanterns in her front window. Kev skipped up the walk and rang the bell.

Old Mrs. Dunbar was a sweet lady and as always she made a big fuss, taking five minutes or so to marvel at the creativity of our costumes. "Jennifer, you look so *cute*! Oh, and look at Hopalong Cassidy over here!"

Kev said, "Hoppy who?"

Old Mrs. Dunbar squinted at me. "Peter Hastings, is that you?"

"Yes, Ma'am."

"Tsk, tsk." She shook her head and folded her arms in front of her chest. "Peter, are you trying to put one over on me?"

"Excuse me, Mrs. Dunbar?"

"Why, Peter . . . you were just here."

All right, this wasn't funny anymore. Charlie was turning my whole world upside down. The little creep was embarrassing me. And the worst part about it, he was scaring me. I remembered those crazy mirrors in the Haunted House and it hit me. Fat kids become skinny, skinny kids become fat . . . dead kids come alive, living kids die!

Charlie was all I could think about. I couldn't

concentrate on anything else, including Timmy Campbell's fastball. He just about beaned me in the head, and took me right off my feet. I lay there in a daze, seeing stars, waiting for the little birds to start tweeting around my head like a cartoon.

Coach Simon stood over me, blocking out the sun. "Are you all right, son? Shake it off." He helped me to my feet and handed me my helmet. "Take a break, Pete."

I stood in the batter's box dusting off the seat of my pants. I saw Timmy Campbell grinning on the pitcher's mound, his team patting him on the back. I felt sick.

Kev was holding down second base. "Are you okay, Pete?"

"Yeah, I'm fine." I took off to the locker room to splash some water on my face. I stared into the mirror and tried to concentrate. "Charlie. Where are you, Charlie? Show yourself!"

"Hello, Peter." He appeared over my shoulder.

I spun around to face him. He still had that dang-blasted yo-yo with him. "You're driving me nuts, you know that?" I said angrily.

He was pouting.

"All right," I said. "I'm sorry I called you the

D word."

He smiled a little. "That Timmy Campbell kid isn't nearly as good as he thinks."

"You kidding me? His fastball's murder!"

"He couldn't strike *me* out."

I suddenly had a thought. "Prove it."

Now it was *his* turn to look puzzled. "Huh?"

"You be me," I said. "Go out there and show him what you have."

He seemed to like that. "For real?"

"For real. You already went trick-or-treating in my place and made Mrs. Dunbar think I'm a pig."

He got that pouting look again. "I'd never been trick-or-treating before. It's fun."

I grabbed the yo-yo out of his hands. "Then, when you're done with Timmy Campbell, you can take my math test for me on Monday. What do you say?"

He looked suddenly unsure. "I don't know."

"C'mon, you want to live my life, don't you?"

He was silent for a bit. Then smiling, he said, "Where's your bat?"

I hid in the stands watching as Charlie stepped into the batter's box wearing my uniform, Number 18. He took a few practice swings, ignoring one of Timmy Campbell's buddies who was yammering, "Hey, batter-batter!"

Timmy Campbell wound up, bringing his shoulders in, and threw his weight behind the pitch. I watched it sail, arcing through the air at the speed of light.

Charlie planted his feet firmly and let it come. He swung. Crack! It sounded like a snapping tree limb. I blinked, and the ball was gone, lost in the stratosphere. I had to resist the urge to clap, in case anyone saw me.

It got to be great fun to fool people, to be in two places at once. All Charlie wanted, I realized, was to have been a kid, to experience the same things other kids did.

No one knew the difference. At first.

The weekend I was supposed to go to Grandma's house but wanted to go camping with Kev and Jennifer instead, Charlie went in my place. The following Monday Grandma spoke to Mom. "Pete wasn't quite himself this weekend."

"What do you mean, Mom?"

"Well, normally he's so well-behaved, so sweet, but this weekend . . . "

I was listening over the phone in my bedroom.

Grandma was saying, "He was all over the place. He let the bird out of its cage, the cat went crazy and knocked over the lamp your sister Sadie gave me. It's in a thousand pieces. He was just uncontrollable."

"You let Grandma's bird out of its cage, and now *I'm* in trouble for it!"

Charlie sat on my bed doing walking-the-dog with Grandpa's yo-yo.

"Why'd you do it?"

"Shhh..." He smiled at me. "You don't want them to catch you talking to yourself again, do you?"

I was beside myself, I was so angry. "You're messing things up for me, Charlie! You got almost every single problem wrong on Mrs. Wallace's math test! She might flunk me now!"

"Well, you should have taken it yourself then," Charlie said. "Serves you right for being lazy."

"How could you get almost every single problem wrong? Are you stupid or something?"

He stopped smiling and his eyes turned cold. "No. I'm just...*dead*."

And with that, he disappeared.

## 9

I was grounded for about a week, and when it was over, I had a terrible case of cabin fever. I hungered to get outside, to see my friends... only my friends didn't want to see me.

Kev started to slam the door in my face, but I stopped it with my foot. "What's wrong with you?"

"I got detention today because of you!"

"What are you talking about? We didn't even see each other at school today."

Kev stood in the doorway tapping his foot, his arms folded across his chest. "You were peeking in the door today when I was in Biology class. You were making faces and you got me laughing. It was the third time this week, and Mr. Stewart wrote me up. I've got detention now all next week."

"Kev, it wasn't me!"

"Well, who was it then? Your twin?"

He slammed the door closed, and I walked home with my head down. And like always, just when you think things couldn't get worse...what happens? They get worse.

I knew something bad had happened the minute I walked in the door. Mom and Dad were sitting in the living room waiting for me, and they didn't look pleased.

"What'd he do now?" I asked.

They stared at me like I was just totally deranged. "What?"

I rephrased the question. "I mean what did *I* do now?"

Mom sat on the edge of the sofa, her lip twitching with rage. "I am so disappointed in you, Peter. Mrs. Russo called this afternoon." That was Gina's mom. "She said you knocked Gina down today and called her a name...a name...I don't even want to repeat that word!"

Dad towered over me and said, "Peter, what did I tell you about fighting? You don't fight with girls, you don't fight with anybody! And *where are* you learning this language?"

What language? This wasn't such a goof anymore.

I was lying in bed that night, sent to my room, probably for all eternity. Kev hated me, Gina hated me, my own family wasn't crazy about me, and I was flunking math. I was beginning to wish Charlie had been the one to live. He'd taken over my life anyway. It might as well be his.

As if in answer to my thoughts, Charlie appeared on the edge of my bed, dangling that yo-yo from his wrist. I was starting to hate the sight of that yo-yo.

"It's okay, Peter," he said. "I got you into this mess, I'll get you out."

I sat up in bed. "But how?"

"Simple. I'll take your place, just like we've been doing. I'll take the heat for you, kid."

I stiffened, that icy feeling crawling up my spine again. "You mean . . . ?"

He smiled coldly. "And *you* can have the yo-yo from now on. It'll be like a trade, but no trade-backs."

Dead kids come alive, living kids die.

# 10

I dialed Kev's number, praying Mr. or Mrs. Wellburn wouldn't answer. It was late. Miraculously, Jennifer picked it up. "Hello?"

"Jen, it's Peter."

"Peter, I was on the other line with Gina." She

sounded grim.

"Look, Jen," I said. "I need help. Remember you said your Aunt Wanda sometimes holds seances, she contacts people's dead relatives and stuff like that?"

"Yeah?"

"Well, I need her help. *Tonight*! It's important!"

"What is?"

"I can't explain over the phone. Can you guys get out of the house?"

"It's almost ten."

I pleaded with her. "Please, Jennifer! It's a matter of life and death!"

There was a long pause, then she took pity on me. "Meet us at Fletcher Park."

I dressed quickly and shimmied down the old oak outside my window. I didn't have much time. I hunched my shoulders against the cold. Winter was coming. I jammed my hands into the pockets of my windbreaker and felt Charlie's yo-yo. He'd left it with me.

Kev and Jennifer were waiting for me at the entrance to Fletcher Park. They had their bikes with them. Kev wouldn't look at me.

"Why don't you guys make up?" Jennifer mildly suggested.

"He's just going to get us both in trouble this time," Kev said.

"Come on." Jennifer nudged him with her shoulder.

I held out my hand to shake. Kev rolled his eyes and took it. "All right," he said. "What's this about?"

"I'll explain it on the way."

Kev looked down at his bike. "I had to sneak this out of the house, you know?"

"You might lose it forever," I said.

He shrugged. "Probably. After tonight, we'll all be grounded until we're fifty. Might as well make an adventure out of it. Hop on."

And we were off. Jennifer rode her bike and I rode on the back of Kev's. Aunt Wanda lived about fifteen minutes away, not far from the fairgrounds. She had an old house at the end of a cul-de-sac on Culver Road. She was sitting on her front porch waiting for us. She already knew!

We sat around a table in Aunt Wanda's basement, holding hands. Her eyes were closed, and in the flickering candlelight, she called Charlie's name.

"Charlie," she said. "Come to us, Charlie."

My eyes scanned the room, looking for any and all signs of him. Nothing.

"Charlie? Speak to us, Charlie."

"It's not fair! There's not supposed to be any trade-backs!"

Charlie was standing in the doorway holding my catcher's mitt, wringing it in his hands like it was his last connection to life. Maybe it was.

Jennifer's mouth was hanging open. "Peter, that's you!"

"No, it's not," Kev whispered. "It's Charlie."

Aunt Wanda opened her eyes and let go of my hand. She turned in her seat and motioned to Charlie with an outstretched palm.

"You have to let go, Charlie," she said. "You have to move on. Peter is the only one who can live his life. No one else."

Charlie's lips quivered. "There's not supposed to be any trade-backs."

Aunt Wanda said, "This isn't a game, Charlie. It's Peter's life, and you have to give it back to him. You have to go on to the other side. You can be at peace there."

Charlie looked like he was going to cry. "But I'm *not* at peace!"

124

"You *can* be, Charlie. You can be."

"I saved his life! I saved him so I could live!"

Aunt Wanda rose from the table and began walking toward Charlie. "I think you saved him that day because you really love him and didn't want anything bad to happen to him."

Charlie lowered his head, loosening his grip on the catcher's mitt and dangling it by the side of his thigh.

Aunt Wanda bent her knees and lowered herself to Charlie's height. "What about Grandpa?" she said. "You have something Peter doesn't have. You can be with your grandfather."

Charlie looked up, and I saw something of a smile crease his face. "Grandpa," he repeated.

Aunt Wanda had tears in her eyes. "You may live again yet, Charlie...but not as Peter."

The room grew very still. Silent. Then Charlie fixed me with his gaze, nodded and held out my catcher's mitt. I was frozen to my seat.

Aunt Wanda looked back at me. "You're the only one who can take it, Peter."

I rose from the table and approached, taking the yo-yo from the pocket of my windbreaker. Grandpa's vintage Forrester. Charlie's yo-yo. I offered it to him in my outstretched hand.

"I'll never forget you, Charlie," I said.

He smiled and took the yo-yo, handing me off my catcher's mitt in the same motion. "No trade-backs," he said.

And he was gone.

We never discussed it again after that night, Kev, Jennifer and I. Aunt Wanda piled their bikes in the back of her station wagon and drove us all home, where we all slept like logs.

The last thing Aunt Wanda said to me was: "Life is for the living, Peter." The same way Charlie had to learn to let go, I had to learn to let *him* go.

Sometime around Christmas, Mom announced she was going to have another baby. Nine months later, my baby sister Charlena was born. Maybe Aunt Wanda was right when she said Charlie may have a life of his own yet. In a sense.

Oh, I did manage to pass math, even hit one of Timmy Campbell's fastballs out of the park on my own once or twice. The only thing—that dang-blasted white streak in my hair. I guess Mrs. Wellburn was onto something after all.

# Something's in the Sewer

**by Shannon Donnelly**

## 1

"Mom, are there alligators in the sewer?" Robbie called out. I tried to catch him and slip my hand across his mouth, but he wiggled out of my reach. He ran into the kitchen and I ran after him.

Mom looked up as we thumped across the wood floor.

"Are there?" Robbie whined. "Tony said there are. He's trying to scare me."

Mom gave me her "I'm-tired-of-this" look. If I

didn't watch it, I'd be the one to get double chores this weekend.

"I didn't say alligators," I said, looking at Robbie as fiercely as I could with Mom watching. I'd put peanut butter in the little creep's shoes if he didn't shut up soon.

"What's an alligator, Mom?" Robbie said, wrapping his arm around her.

Mom put a hand down to smooth his brown hair, which is always sticking up. My hair is black like Mom's and never does anything but lie flat like it was dead. Then she turned away and tore open a package of frozen green stuff. "It's a kind of lizard and there aren't any in the sewer. Tony, I wish you would stop making up stories to torment your brother and..."

"I didn't say alligators, Mom."

"...and put that imagination of yours to better use in school."

Slumping into a chair, I got ready for her "active imagination" speech. I heard it a lot from Mom and Dad. I still hadn't figured out if it was a good thing. A kid in school—Susan May—had to leave and go to another school because she was active. Hyperactive, the teacher said. I wasn't sure if that's the same kind of active my parents talk about. But if it means that your mind makes up stuff and pictures just pop into your head, then, yeah, I guess I had one.

Mom talked and I sat there and said, "Yes, Mom," when she asked a question, but I wasn't really listening.

I told Robbie about the sewers because I didn't want him to go near that corner. Of course, he got it all wrong. And Mom wouldn't listen. I could just see her face getting that blank look if I told her, "Mom, there's something in the sewers. I haven't seen it, but I can smell it and it smells like watermelon sour candy and that rotten Easter egg Robbie never found last year until it was June. And I can hear it. I hear it slurping down in the drains like it's eating something. I hear it when I'm walking to school, like it's following me. I can hear it trying to squish out of the drain like ketchup that's trying to come out of the squeeze-bottle."

Yeah, she'd really believe all that.

The trouble was that I wasn't even sure I believed it.

Maybe it was just my imagination. Make-believe stuff. I had lived here all my life and had never seen anything strange before. I had never heard anything, until this year when school started. Maybe that was why an imagination was bad if it was active—maybe it made up too much stuff.

"Are you listening to me, young man?"

I looked up. Mom stood right in front of me. In her hands, she had a white pot with the frozen green block sticking up. She looked angry. I felt my face go hot and splotchy. "Yeah, sure. Uh, do you want me to pour the milk for dinner?" I got up and started for the fridge before she could answer.

Dinner was meat loaf and green beans. I chopped up my meat loaf into small brown bits and mixed them in the beans so Mom would think I had eaten some. I kept thinking about what I had heard and smelled from the sewers.

Maybe I had only heard some gunk going down the drains. Everyone dumped stuff down the sewer drains. Car oil, leaves, stuff out of the trash can. I had even seen a dirty white high-top wash down the drains last winter. But that stuff splashed and thudded when it got washed down. None of that stuff ever slurped like someone eating hot soup.

After dinner, Mom made me get my homework done. Dad helped me with math, which I hate. Then we watched a cop show on TV with a lot of fast cars and guys running up and down stairs. I forgot about the sewer until I lay down in my bed with the light off. The wind blew hard, making a branch tap on my window.

Tap. Tap. Tap. It sounded like a code. Tap. Tap-tap. Tap. It sounded like water dripping in a big empty sewer drain. Tap. Tap. Tap-tap. It sounded like the running footsteps of someone trying to get out of a sewer drain, and get away from "something."

I woke to hear Mom calling for Robbie and me to get up. My eyes felt like someone had glued them shut. I struggled out of the warm sheets and slid off my pajamas. After splashing cold water on my face, I pulled on a clean pair of jeans and a black sweatshirt from my drawer.

"Don't think that dragging your tail around here is going to get you off going to school today," Mom said as I yawned my way into the kitchen.

I looked up at her and rubbed the sleepy-bits from my eyes. "You want me to make Robbie's lunch?" I asked, grabbing for a banana. The floor felt really cold on my feet, so I stood with one foot held up and moved from foot to foot.

She nodded, pouring coffee for herself and Dad. She had on her nice clothes so I knew she'd be busy today.

I took fifteen minutes to get the mayonnaise spread just right on Robbie's bread. I ate the banana and watched the big kitchen clock as I worked to try and make it take even more time. Then I threw away the banana peel and got out the ham package. I put the ham on, one slice at a time, making kind of a star with the slices. I tried to stretch out the time before I hit that corner as long as I could.

Dad came in, gave this big sigh and took everything away from me. "Just finish getting dressed. I'll give you two a ride to school today."

Yes! I pounded up the stairs and had my socks and shoes on in two minutes!

"Can you pick us up today?" I asked as he dropped me off in front of my playground. We had already dropped Robbie off at his preschool, the one with the circus animals painted on the walls. I gave Dad a big smile, and rubbed the silver handle on the car.

"I can't, buddy. I've got to show a house today. Robbie's going over to Mrs. Patterson's after preschool, so I want you to go straight home. And page me as soon as you get there. Now be good. And see if you can learn something today." He smiled and leaned over the seat to lock the car door. Walking to class, I kicked at rocks and clumps of grass.

School ended too early. The bell rang and the other kids ran out but I sat at my desk. I dug my fingernail into a scratch that someone had made in the wood. A sliver dug into my skin and I had to pull it out. Mr. Arnold looked at me through his silver glasses and asked if anything was wrong. So I asked him if he needed erasers cleaned or anything.

Thumping erasers kept me busy for half an hour. I made these cool patterns by throwing the erasers onto the blacktop. I made a car, and a bridge, and then a horse—only its head came out square because you can't do circles very well with straight erasers. I smelled like chalk by the time Mr. Arnold came out. He said I had done a good enough job and maybe I should go home now.

So I asked Mr. Arnold if he wanted to give me a ride. He laughed and talked about how far he had to walk to school as a kid. I didn't see why that meant that I had to walk too, but I knew he wasn't going to let me ride home in his station wagon. I slumped off down the street, heading for that corner.

When I turned onto Orchard, I started walking slower. The wind tugged at my jacket and stung my cheeks. I could smell wood fires and I wished that I was at home in front of one.

Fifth and Orchard looked like any other street corner. Almost. I had seen most of the other street corners around here when I tried to find a way to school that didn't take me past Fifth and Orchard. There wasn't any other way. All the streets around my house wound around and turned into each other or ended in a big circle. The only street that went through was Orchard. And that street crossed Fifth.

Fifth and Orchard.

I had started to hate the sound of those two street names.

I squinted up at the sky. The trees were almost bare. A few leaves clung to the branches like they were afraid to let go. I thought they looked like bits of paper bag that someone had tied to the white twists of branches. They looked like warning flags. Like someone had put them up there to tell people to stay away.

Above the trees, puffs of clouds flew across the sky. I wished that I could ride on a cloud. That would be cool. I'd be home in two seconds and look down at Fifth and Orchard and I wouldn't hear anything or smell anything.

I kept my head back so long that my neck began to ache.

Looking up at the sky, I tried to see cloud-shapes. I whistled and thought about anything but a slurping sound. Maybe it wouldn't happen if I didn't make it happen in my mind.

It got harder to whistle as I got closer to the corner. My mouth dried up. My steps slowed. My feet felt heavy like someone had put glue on the street to make my shoes stick. I wet my lips and looked at the street.

The corner of Fifth and Orchard had four stop signs. Under each red sign with its white letters, was a drain cut into the sidewalk. Four signs, four drains. The drains looked like slits. They gaped open without even a metal bar to keep stuff from falling inside and washing away. They looked wide enough, and just tall enough, for a kid about my height and size to fall down one of them. Fall down and never get out.

No matter which side of the street I used, I

had to walk right past one of the drains. Under my jacket, I shivered.

Hardly any cars ever came this way. The school bus drove past, but we lived so close that the bus didn't stop for kids in my neighborhood. I wished that it did. I wished that I could ride the bus past my house and get off and walk back from the other side of town. But the guy who drove the school bus wouldn't let me do that again. He had caught me the week before and said that he would be looking for me.

I wished I had a bike that I could ride really fast. A blue mountain bike with streamers on the handlebars. Or skates. Black, in-line skates with purple wheels. Or a skateboard. Glow-in-the-dark green with a cool sticker on it. Or anything that would let me go faster.

Walking sideways, I edged over toward the sidewalk edge.

Usually, I looked both ways first, for cars. Then I ran as fast as I could down the center of the street. Only I wasn't so sure that was safe anymore. Last week, the slurping sound had moved really fast. Faster than I could run. And, as my foot hit the metal sewer drain cap in the middle, I had felt the cap lift a little. Like something pushed it up.

No, I wasn't so sure the middle of the street was safe. But I had to get home somehow.

I looked back, down Orchard, and didn't see any cars. I looked forward, up Orchard, and didn't see any cars. I stepped off the curb and got ready to run.

That's when I spotted the other kid.

## 2

He sat in the dirt on an empty lot. The lot wasn't wide enough for a house. It was between two other houses, the one on the corner and the other one on its other side. The lot was just a thin strip of dirt with some metal boxes. The boxes had the word DANGER painted on them in blocky black letters. I think the boxes were for the sewer.

The boy sat just behind a wall that separated the empty lot from the one next to it. I would have seen him sooner, but he leaned against the wall so that he faced the corner.

He had light brown hair about Robbie's color, only his hair curled instead of standing up. He wore wire glasses like Mr. Arnold's. He looked about my age. He sat with his feet on the ground and his knees up, as if ready to get up really quick. He had on jeans, a blue shirt and a plastic windbreaker. He balanced a notepad on his knees.

Then I saw where he was staring.

He hadn't seen me because he was staring at the corner. Like he couldn't ever look away. I looked to where he was staring. Straight at the steel drain cover in the middle of the street.

He knew.

He knew about it. He wouldn't be watching the sewer if he hadn't heard it or smelled it like I had.

I walked over to him. He didn't look up even though I scuffed my sneakers against the sidewalk. The sneakers hadn't cost much and scuffing them left bits of white plastic on the cement. When I was right next to him, I stopped. He knew that I was there because he shifted on the dirt like he felt funny having someone watch him.

"What do you think it is?" I asked.

He looked up at me real quick. Then he looked back at the sewer drains. He didn't seem to mind that I hadn't even asked his name. "I don't know, yet. You ever see it?"

I hunkered down beside him, squatting on my heels. "I smelled it—sweet and sticky. It smells like it's been down there too long."

Looking down, he wrote in his notebook. I tried to see what he had written, but he printed small, tight letters that you could hardly see.

Then he said, "I saw it. Yesterday."

I looked up from trying to read his writing. He had gray eyes behind the glasses. He had freckles across his nose and really pale skin like he didn't get outside much.

"You've seen it?" I said. I couldn't help it, that I sounded like I didn't believe him. I didn't want to believe him. I didn't want to think that it could get out of the sewer long enough to be seen. It was bad enough smelling it and hearing it. I shivered and pulled my jacket closed.

He nodded and looked back at the sewer. "But I don't know what it is. It's just *something*."

My feet had started to ache, so I twisted to sit down beside him. "Do you think it . . . " I stopped. Had I heard something? Maybe just the wind. Keeping my voice low, I asked, "What do you think it eats?"

He shook his head. "Not sure. It might just be a mold, or a fungus. You know, like a mushroom."

I'd never heard of a mushroom that moved. I didn't say anything though. It might just be something that grew in sewers and never came out of the drains. I wanted to hang on to that idea.

We sat there for a while. I didn't talk. I was too busy listening. I thought I had heard it again. That slurping. It sounded like a straw does when you've run out of drink and still suck on the straw. What did *it* suck on?

I looked up. The sky wasn't blue anymore. It was turning dark gray.

"It's getting dark," I said and stood up. I stamped my feet to get the blood moving.

The other boy nodded and got up. "What do you think is down there?"

I stared at the sewer drain. I didn't want to tell him what I thought hid down there in the sludge and slime. I didn't want to tell anyone. If I gave it a name, it might make it worse. Maybe it would hear and think that I'd tried to call it. I shivered and stuffed my hands into my pockets.

"It's something awful, isn't it," I said, keeping

my voice low just in case it could hear. I felt stupid about doing that. But I also felt scared enough that I didn't mind acting a little dumb about some things.

"We have to learn more. That's the scientific way. Any phenomenon can be identified with enough study," he said.

It sounded like he had heard that in a movie or something. He put his pencil in his shirt pocket and closed his notebook. Then he looked at me. "Maybe we should split up. You want to take that side?"

I nodded, understanding his idea. If we split up, we might get past. If it oozed out, it might not know which one of us to get. It wasn't as good as driving past in a car, but it might get us both home.

"Did it sound fast to you?" he asked.

I nodded again. It sounded more than fast. It sounded hungry, almost like a big, hollow, empty stomach grumbling for food.

I jogged across the street. My heart had already started thumping inside me like I'd been running all day. I glanced over at him. He stood with his feet wide apart and his notebook gripped in one hand. He looked ready to start a race. Some race. We didn't even know what we were racing. I guess we'd know if we lost.

He waved and sprinted forward. I ran too. I ran so hard that I almost couldn't hear anything but the wind in my ears and my blood pounding faster than my sneakers. Almost. But I heard the other kid's shoes thudding on the sidewalk. And I heard something else that made me push myself faster.

The slurping oozed along behind me. I heard it running under the street the way I ran above it. I heard it down in the drains, moving around like water sloshing. Only it wasn't water. I knew that because I heard it slurp forward, then stop, as if it had to decide which way to go, and then start sloshing again. It was moving after us.

I saw the other kid running on the sidewalk. He kept as far away from the street and drains as he could. The wind pushed his hair back. I sped up, but he ran faster than I did. His feet flew over the ground, hardly touching. He pulled ahead, arms pumping up and down. His plastic jacket flapped against his back.

Don't leave me. Please, don't leave me. I kept thinking that as I saw him pull ahead. He turned down the next corner, feet still pounding, eyes squinted shut. He disappeared. The sound of his steps faded away. I had to keep going straight ahead to get home.

The cold air stung my face and hurt inside my chest. I had to look back, which made me slow down, but it seemed okay.

Nothing. Not a cat or a dog or a bird moved. I slowed a little more so I could catch my breath. I had to slow down for just a while. Running hard had made my nose run, so I wiped it with my sleeve and sniffed.

Big mistake.

The smell rose up like something dead had been cut open. I choked and scrunched up my face against the stink. My stomach flopped over. I took a deep breath and I held it. Then I turned and started running. My feet got heavy and slow. I tried to go faster, but every step got harder. Too hard.

When I reached the next corner I slowed down. I held my breath for just a moment and listened.

Then I heard something.

Nothing much. Just a little gurgle, like water circling down a tub drain after a bath. A quiet almost-not-there sound. I glanced behind me, but it hadn't come from that way. So where?

Closing my eyes, I listened. I bit my lower lip till it hurt, and listened hard.

A soft slurp. Like gum stuck to pavement and shoe. It came from across the street. From in front of me.

Opening my eyes, I looked and went from burning hot to shivering cold. Another sewer drain split the curb from the street on the corner ahead of me. I'd almost run right over it.

I cut across the street, walking fast. My side ached, so I held it and walked faster. I looked back, and I couldn't see anything. But I smelled it. That rotten, too sweet smell. I broke into a jog.

Did it sound faster, too, like the water had sped up? Was the smell stronger? How fast could it get? How far could it get? Maybe I'd already outrun it and had just imagined that I'd heard it. Could someone imagine smells? I didn't want to slow down and find out.

The wind pushed against my chest and face, making it harder to run, pushing me backward. I could barely lift my feet. Overhead, the streetlights flickered and winked on. I glanced at the houses on either side of the street, all dark and empty, waiting for people to come home from work. I slowed down again to listen, and swallow my heart which kept jumping up into my throat. For a second, I thought I'd beat it. Then I looked ahead and saw the next sewer drain.

Had I heard something in that drain, too? A quiet, lapping sound? Did "something" hide there, quiet and waiting? Could it be that smart?

Crossing the street at a run, I leaped and landed in someone's yard so that I didn't even have to step in the gutter that led to the sewer. I kept running on the grass. I jumped hedges. I struggled over walls. I tripped on a hose and fell face-down on the grass and lay there, my chest aching. The wind rattled the bare tree branches, hiding other sounds. Dragging myself up, I kept going until I got home.

As I staggered up the drive, I looked over my shoulder. I kept hearing that sick slurping, but I couldn't tell if I really heard it, or if I just couldn't stop hearing it. I knew I'd hear that sound in my dreams.

But I didn't want it following me home, like some stray thing. I didn't want it to know where I lived. Maybe it couldn't get here. Maybe it had given up. It must have.

Just as I stepped onto the walkway to our front door, a loud hiss of water came at me from next door.

I jumped off the path and rolled onto our lawn. I lay there, hands covering my face, listening to the hiss. I couldn't run anymore. I lay there, shaking all over, too scared and frightened to do anything.

Nothing happened.

Slowly, I took my hands off my face. I sat up. The hissing sputtered and started again.

I stood up and peeked over the neighbor's wall. Mrs. Bailey's automatic sprinklers had come on.

I walked back to our house, looking over my shoulder just in case. I pulled the key out from the hanging flower pot where Mom hides it. Wet dirt stuck to my fingers and made them smell like the fishy stuff Mom feeds to the plants. I let myself in. I called Dad's pager as I looked in the fridge for milk and something to eat. He called me back right away.

"You're late calling," he said, his voice sounding funny, like he was calling from the car.

"Sorry. I stayed to help Mr. Arnold clean erasers. Dad, what's *fa-nom-a-nun* mean?"

"It means something that hardly ever happens—like you doing anything other than daydreaming. Look it up in the dictionary, it's spelled with a 'p-h.' I'll pick up Robbie and dinner on my way home. Pizza okay with you?"

The next morning, I saw the other kid at school. He was lined up to go into Mrs. Ferman's class. I hadn't noticed him before because he wasn't in my class and he looked the same as a lot of the other kids. He was skinnier than me, and tall. Taller than almost everyone, and everyone's taller than I am. At recess, I went to Mrs. Ferman's classroom. It smelled like chalk and old schoolbooks.

The kid stood near the windows on the other side of the room. Two big glass jars sat on a counter in front of him. He had an eyedropper in one hand.

He saw me and waved for me to come in. "Want to feed my ants?"

I walked over. The big jars had more in them than dirt. I saw black dots crawling around inside one, carving tunnels against the glass. The one on the left was just as big but it had red dots. I leaned down to look closer. "What do you feed them?"

"Sugar water." He unscrewed the top of one

jar and squeezed the eyedropper over the dirt. The ants swarmed over the drops like Robbie on top of Christmas presents. The jars had labels on the front.

"Family Fo-mi-ci-dae," I read, sounding out the word the way Dad had taught me. It also had a date and a name, Sheldon Lemic. "Are you Sheldon?" I asked, straightening.

He nodded. "Ants belong to the same order as wasps and bees."

"Order? I thought that's something you did at McDonald's."

He looked at me, then he laughed. "It's like to put in order. Bees and wasps and ants all belong to the same group. They're all the same kind of insects."

I looked at him from the corner of my eye. "How do you know all this stuff?"

He shrugged. "I just read a lot."

Opening the other jar, he squeezed the eyedropper over it. The liquid dropped in and the ants went crazy picking up the drops. "Close it, will you?" he asked. "They got out last week and Mrs. Ferman said that if they get out again, I'm going to have to do an experiment that's less trouble."

148

Picking up the top, I screwed it back on. "Where did you read all this stuff about ants?" I asked. I leaned down and watched them hurry around.

"I got a book out of the library." He pointed to the label. "That's where I got this stuff from." He grinned suddenly. "I'm not really that smart. I just know how to use the library."

I looked at him. "Do you think they have a book on sewers?"

We went to the library after school. I phoned Mom from a pay phone outside and she said she'd pick Sheldon and me up after she finished work. She sounded happy that I was with another kid, and at the library without her having to drag me there to finish an overdue book report. It wasn't that I didn't like the place. I somehow always ended up lost in the rows of books, and then Mom would get mad when she found me in the science-fiction section with some story that wasn't on my book report list.

Today, Sheldon dragged me over to a computer terminal before I could wander anywhere. "We can search magazines for articles. We need something printed not too long ago."

I nodded. "It wasn't there last year."

"Yeah, I know. What do you think we should search for?"

That part was easy. "Garbage. Sewer. Car oil. Shoes. Tires." I named the other stuff I had seen go down the sewer. Sheldon looked at me kind of funny, like he thought I was joking about it all. I guess the way I looked told him I wasn't laughing at any of this.

Sheldon added a few words of his own. Science, biology and some others I didn't know. He wrote down the names of the magazines that the computer found, and the names of the articles. Then we went to the librarian.

She looked at the list, then she looked at us with her mouth scrunched up, like we were making too much work for her.

"Science project," Sheldon said, tapping the eraser of his pencil on the counter.

I nodded. "Yeah. For school."

The librarian left. I started to wander over to some paperback books, but Sheldon pulled me away. The librarian came back with a stack of magazines. We got three each—our limit—and she told us that when we finished these, we could swap them for the others we wanted to see.

An hour later, I was bored.

I had lost count of how many magazines I had read. Ink had come off on my fingers, leaving them black and smelly.

I had read about alligators in Florida's sewers. Only I didn't live in Florida and this wasn't an alligator. I read about treating sewage to get water out of it. I read about sneakers getting washed off Japanese ships and floating to Oregon. I read in a local newspaper about how our town was built on a landfill—a place where lots of garbage was dumped and then covered with dirt. I hadn't read anything about something that smelled and lived in sewers.

I was ready for Mom to pick us up. I walked over to Sheldon.

He looked up and I wasn't ready to go anymore.

I felt cold.

Sheldon's eyes looked really bright. He had found something.

"Listen to this!" He pointed to an article with a picture of an oil well and started reading. "Scientists now believe they have developed micro-organisms that..."

"Micro-what?"

Sheldon looked up at me. "Real small things. You know, microbes."

"Oh."

He started reading again. "...microorganisms that can digest oil, using enzymes that can be adapted for..."

"En-what?"

He put down the magazines. "Small things that eat oil. Now, do you want to hear this?"

"Yeah, I was just asking." I sat down in the chair next to him.

"Adapted for..." he ran a finger down the typed print, "...other purposes. With genetic-engineering..." Sheldon paused and looked at me. "That's something weird that scientists do. Anyway, what this says is that people create these things to eat oil—and to eat garbage."

I thought about that, then said, "Yeah, but whatever is in the sewer doesn't sound like it's really small."

"What if it got bigger?" Sheldon closed the magazine and twisted around to face me. "What if it had so much garbage to eat that it *could* get really big? What if *all* it did was eat garbage and get bigger? Like a shark does, only it's not a shark?"

My chair felt too hard suddenly. I wiggled to make it feel softer. "I have to show you something." I went to my pile of magazines. I found the newspaper with the stuff about the town being built on a landfill. Sheldon read it twice as fast as I had.

Then he looked up. "That's it. I'll bet it's been down there for years. Goldfish get really big if you put them in a big pond and feed them a lot. They can get giant." He spread out his hands to show me.

I swallowed. My stomach hurt. How big could a goldfish get in a sewer? How big could these microbe things get?

Sheldon kept talking, his voice fast and getting kind of squeaky. "Maybe it's been getting fat on all the garbage and oil and junk dumped down the drains. Maybe it just keeps getting bigger and bigger."

"Maybe," I said, "it wants something better to eat than garbage."

Sheldon looked at me. His face was real pale.

Light bounced off his glasses for a second, filling them up. Then I met his stare. He didn't like the idea any more than I did.

I heard Mom's honk. We grabbed the magazines and stuffed them at the librarian. We didn't want to miss our ride past Fifth and Orchard. Not tonight. Not ever.

Robbie got me a ride to school the next morning. He wasn't feeling well and when Mom took his temperature, it read one hundred. So she called the doctor and dropped me off on the way to take Robbie to see him. I felt bad being happy that Robbie was sick. Not that I wanted him sick. But it meant that I didn't have to walk past it. So I told Robbie that he could play some of my videotapes that afternoon if he wanted to.

I ate lunch with Sheldon and we talked about the sewer.

"Maybe it only eats garbage," Sheldon said.

I chewed my cafeteria pizza. The cheese pulled off in long white threads that looked like someone's skin peeling off. The tomato sauce smelled spicy, but it looked like blood. The bread lay white as a bone under everything. I wasn't feeling too cheerful. I put the pizza down and dug into the chocolate pudding. That wasn't any better. My spoon pulled out with a sucking noise, like how it would sound if your foot got caught in something slimy and you tried to pull it out.

I pushed my lunch tray away. "What do ants eat, besides sugar water?"

Sheldon shrugged. "Almost anything."

"What about sharks? Don't they eat garbage?" I had read in one of the magazines at the library about a shark getting cut open and people finding tin cans and old boots inside it. "And almost anything else?"

Sheldon nodded.

"Sharks eat people, too," I said.

Sheldon looked down at his lunch tray. Then he looked up. "Want to walk home together today?"

I nodded.

I met him at the school gate. We didn't talk much. I don't think he wanted to say what he was thinking any more than I did.

It was getting darker a little earlier every day. Winter was coming. The sun disappeared by four in the afternoon. I was glad Sheldon was walking with me.

In some ways, it made it better that I had

someone else who knew it was there. In some ways, it made it all worse. I couldn't pretend anymore that I had just made up everything in my mind. The sounds. The smell. They weren't at all make-believe.

"What's it look like?" I asked finally.

Sheldon dug his hand into his jacket pocket so that his fist made a lump. "It looks weird. You know how you kind of see colors when sunlight hits an oily street after a rain? It's like that—all black and shiny, but with colors sort of rippling through the way they make flavors swirl through ice cream. But the light isn't like sunlight shining on something . . . it's like . . . it's like the light is coming from inside. From inside in those circle-patterns that make it look like something sparkling."

"Like blinking colored lights?" I asked, my steps slowing.

Sheldon nodded.

I pointed ahead to the corner of Fifth and Orchard at the oil-slick blacktop that glistened there.

"Does it look like that?"

# 4

When we stopped walking, I heard the slurping. It was close. Too close. The smell oozed up around us like we had stepped on rotten eggs and bits of sour candies. The smell left a taste in my mouth, a dry, sour taste like the metal around a pencil eraser.

Ahead, the street glistened slightly. Only there wasn't any sunlight to make it shine. The clouds hung low over us, pressing down like we were inside a dirty gray tent. It hadn't rained, but the street right around the sewer drains looked slick and wet. Only the air didn't smell clean, like after a rain. It smelled sour and old.

I looked at Sheldon. My mouth felt dry, as if I had eaten too many soda crackers. Sheldon didn't look at me. He started walking forward, his eyes bright again. I swallowed the dry feeling in my mouth and followed one step behind him, pulling my jacket close around me.

The sidewalk felt funny, like walking on a plastic trash bag. I couldn't really see anything but pavement under my feet and that shiny, slick stuff right near the drain mouths.

Suddenly, Sheldon turned to me. "Come on!" He grabbed my arm, pulling at my jacket. Then he let go and he started to run.

I ran too. I didn't ask why. I didn't need to. I could hear the slurping, gurgling coming out of the drains.

We cut out into the middle of the street. The sound got louder as we passed the drains. I didn't look at them. I closed my eyes and put my head back. My arms pumped at my sides and my legs pounded. Fast-ter. Fast-ter. *Fast-ter*, I thought, my feet smacking so hard against the ground that it stung. I liked the hard hammering under my feet. Anything but stepping on that soft, slick stuff.

I heard Sheldon's feet just in front of me and to my left. Behind us, I heard a metal clink, like something had picked up the sewer drain cover in the middle of the street and let it fall again.

Then we were past. Past all four drains. Past the sound. But I smelled that sweet sticky smell all the way home.

Mom had stayed home that day to look after Robbie, who was feeling better enough to whine that he didn't feel good. As I stepped inside, warm air washed over me, making my face burn after having been so cold.

Mom yelled for me to wash up when I slammed through the front door, panting for breath. "And pour the milk for dinner when you've washed," she yelled from upstairs. I heard Robbie complain that he wanted to come downstairs to eat and I knew that Mom must be up in his room.

Yanking off my jacket, I ran water over my hands and wiped my palms on my jeans. Mom's cooking filled the kitchen with good smells.

I pulled the milk carton out of the fridge and saw my hands shake. I had to hold the carton with both hands to keep from spilling it.

After I poured the glasses, I put my elbows on the table and my chin in my hands and stared at the milk carton. I tried to make my heart stop beating so fast.

Maybe I should tell Mom and Dad about it. Maybe they would start taking me to school if I told them.

I stared at the milk carton, wondering what I should do.

I don't know why I hadn't seen it before. I guess, like Mom says, I don't pay attention sometimes. My mind takes off in its own world. But now, the words and picture on the milk carton jumped out at me like they were in 3-D.

Missing.

One big, black word at the top, just under the blue label that read MILK. Then a kid's picture. Then the other words.

Last seen near Fifth and Orchard.

Then came a lot of stuff about the kid, a girl with a front tooth missing and long hair tied back with a ribbon. I got up and pulled out the other cartons. The glossy cardboard felt slick in my hands and I almost dropped one.

The next carton had the girl's picture again. The third had a boy's picture. He was Robbie's age and had really short hair and sandy eyebrows that almost weren't there. All the cartons with the missing kids' pictures said, "Last seen near Fifth and Orchard." How many? How many had it got? Had it almost got me and Sheldon tonight?

I put the milk cartons back into the fridge. Then I sat down at the dinner table again.

Mom came into the kitchen looking tired. I wasn't going to say anything to her before dinner. But she ruffled my hair and said that she had made tacos for me for dinner, and the words just started spilling out from me like pennies from a busted piggy bank.

"...and then we ran and it smelled really bad and Sheldon read this stuff about micro-things that eat stuff and all these other kids are missing there and..." I heard it coming out, but I couldn't stop talking. I couldn't even slow down the words or make them sound good. They just poured out of me until I was empty. Then I sat there staring at Mom so hard that my eyes started to water.

Mom sat down and put beef crumbs into a taco shell, then stuffed lettuce and cheese on top. "Tony." She shook her head and smiled, but her eyes still looked tired. "I wish you'd put even half of this energy and imagination into your school work. Now, sit down and eat before it gets cold."

I sat. But I didn't eat much. Mom felt my forehead. She said that she hoped that I wasn't getting what Robbie had and sent me to bed early.

I got into my pajamas and brushed with my mint-flavored toothpaste. After I sloshed water around my mouth, I put away my toothbrush and turned to use the toilet.

I stood there, staring at the white toilet.

Reaching out, I pushed the silver handle

down. The water circled, it gurgled, it sloshed down the drain.

Down the drain and into the sewer.

Could something that goes down into the sewer come back up? I backed away from the toilet. If it could make itself into a thin goo on the street, could it squeeze through pipes and come up drains?

I looked at the water tap over the sink, then at the bathtub drain, then at the faucet into the bathtub, then at the sink drain and back to the toilet. It could squeeze up anywhere. I thought about the kitchen sink, the dishwasher.

Anywhere.

A bubble of air came up in the toilet.

I slammed the toilet lid down and ran out of the bathroom with the door banging shut behind me.

That night I had nightmares about shiny, gooey things and missing children and stuff oozing its way up the toilet and into my bathroom.

The next day at lunch I told Sheldon about the kids and the milk cartons. I thought about telling him about the toilet, but I felt stupid talking about that. We hadn't heard the Something anywhere but in the sewer at Fifth and Orchard. The smell only came up out of the drains there. We had only almost seen it there. Maybe it couldn't get anywhere else. Maybe.

Sheldon ate his tuna sandwich and potato chips while I talked. Then the bell rang. Sheldon got up, saying to meet him in his classroom after school, that he had to think.

After school, I slipped into Mrs. Ferman's room as she was at the chalkboard. Sheldon was feeding his ants. He had that look again. That big-eyed look. My stomach did a flip when I saw that look.

"We've got to do something," he said. He glanced at Mrs. Ferman's back, but she hadn't heard. "Something to get rid of it before anyone else is missing."

I nodded and whispered, "What about the kids already gone?"

He frowned. "I don't know." He put the lids back on his ant jars, then he picked up his note-book and said good-bye to Mrs. Ferman. We walked outside and over to the recess play-ground. The air smelled wet.

"We should make a list. We have to figure out how to get rid of it." He sat down on a swing and

I sat on the one next to him. He turned to a new page in his notebook. "Now, what do we know about it?"

I scuffed the toe of my shoe in the sand under the swings, leaving a wiggling line. Some of the sand got into my shoe and rubbed. "It's getting worse," I said.

"Yeah, but why?"

"Because it's winter?" I said, guessing more than knowing.

"Okay, that makes sense, but what happens in winter?"

I shrugged. "School. Shorter days. Holidays. It gets cold."

He printed the small, blocky letters. "Shorter days. That could mean that it doesn't like light."

I nodded. "Yeah, the darker it is, the louder it sounds and the worse it smells."

"But it's colder in winter, too. Maybe it's heat that it doesn't like. It gets hot when it's sunny." He wrote in his notebook. "What else goes on in summer?"

I shrugged. "I don't know."

"Okay, so what else do we know about it then?"

"Well—it sounds like water dripping sometimes. It sounds wet."

"Wet?" He looked up from his notebook. "Yeah, that could be it. Evaporation!" I stared at him. He didn't notice. He just kept talking, his voice fast. "Heat and light can make a liquid dry up. Like the way a puddle disappears in summer."

I turned around in the swing so that the chains twisted around each other with sharp clanks. As I turned, I looked around at the empty playground. The tetherball chains rattled against their metal poles, the balls put away for the night. "Sheldon, we're just guessing. We don't know any of this for sure."

"Of course we do. We know from . . . " he scrunched up his eyes and then said, like he had read this, " . . . from direct observation—that means we've seen it."

"You've seen it. I only almost saw it. But there's a lot of other stuff that happens in summer. Maybe it dries up in summer. But what if something else gets rid of it? What if we're wrong?"

He closed his notebook. "You want to just wait and do nothing? Is that it? You're scared, so you don't want to do anything?" He sounded mad.

I slumped down in the swing. I thought about

the sewer. I thought about the missing kids and that sucking sound from the corner of Fifth and Orchard. I felt cold inside. Cold and shaking and sick. If Mom or Dad had come up to me right then and said that we were moving, I would have been ready to go in five minutes. But I felt stupid telling Sheldon that.

"So what do we do?" I asked, dragging my toe through the sand again.

"We have to try something. You know, like an experiment. We have to try and hit it with light and heat and see if that makes it go away, or makes it smaller. We have to at least see if we can do something about it."

"Hit it?" My voice squeaked as I said that and I had to say it again. Then I said, "Can't we just tell someone about it, and what we think we know about it? Won't that be just as good?"

"You try telling your parents yet?"

Yeah, I had. But I didn't tell Sheldon that. I had even told Robbie again to stay away. Robbie hadn't been listening to me. Someday, he might go walking down Orchard. Maybe one day really late in the day. Even though the little monster made me want to punch him sometimes, I didn't want to see his picture on a milk carton.

Slowly, I nodded. "Okay. When?" I asked, my stomach tying into knots.

His eyes got bright again. "Tomorrow. Just after sunrise and before school."

I got up from the swing and said that I would. We walked home together. When we got to Fifth and Orchard, Sheldon nodded to me and we both ran past, splitting up like we had the other day. I didn't hear it behind us and for a second I wondered if it had just gone away. But I knew it hadn't. I just knew it.

I spent the rest of the day and that night making believe that I hadn't said that I would meet Sheldon.

The next morning came too fast. After I got dressed, Mom said that since I was up early, I should make myself useful. She told me to take out the garbage can onto the street for the trash man to pick up. Then I had to make my bed and put away my toys and the videos that Robbie had messed up.

I felt funny as I worked. I didn't know if I was happy or not to have her keep me home and busy. I felt like I do when I'm at the dentist and other kids keep getting called in before me. I knew it would be my turn, sooner or later. Was it better to be sooner and get it over? Or was later better? If time got too late, maybe I wouldn't have to meet Sheldon.

Mom ran out of chores after I had made a lunch for me and Robbie. Then I had to go.

I got to Fifth and Orchard just as the sun poked over the tops of houses. Garbage cans—some plastic, some metal—stood up along Orchard, waiting for the trash truck to come around. The trees had lost all their leaves and looked dead against the cloudy sky. Brown leaves crunched under my steps. The grass on everyone's lawns looked brown and dead, too.

I didn't see Sheldon, so I slowed down. I felt like someone had just opened a back door to the dentist's office and whispered to me, telling me how to sneak out. I didn't even have to feel bad that I was scared. I wasn't the only one. He must have felt that way, too.

I walked faster. I wanted to get past the corner and get to school. I'd talk to Sheldon at school and we'd make other plans. We could wait until summer to do something. Yeah, that was a good idea. I could see us with ropes and lights and camping lanterns in the summer. Maybe by then, someone else would even notice what was going on.

My daydream about summer ended when I saw the black tube.

The tube lay in the gutter, right in front of the empty lot where I had first seen Sheldon. I walked over to it slowly, like it might get up and bite me. A few big red ants ran over it. I brushed the ants off and picked it up.

It was a flashlight, almost as long as from my elbow to my hand. No one would throw away a flashlight like this. It must have cost a month's allowance. I pushed the squishy black button on the side. Yellow light glowed in the bulb.

Sheldon.

I looked out into the street.

In the center of Fifth and Orchard, the metal sewer drain cover lay next to a round black hole. The cover had come off the hole. And Sheldon had gone down the hole—without his flashlight.

Feet dragging, I walked over to the drain. I couldn't hear any slurping sound, but my heart pounded so hard in my ears that I don't think I would have heard a truck honking right behind me.

Sheldon didn't show up, I told myself. Sheldon didn't move the drain cover. Sheldon didn't drop this flashlight when something dragged him down.

All along, I knew the truth. I had been late. And Sheldon hadn't waited.

My mind made pictures about how the creepy, gooey stuff had been lying on the street, waiting. Waiting for Sheldon to step in it. It sparkled inside, like it had eaten glitter, and waited in the dark morning. Smelling foul and sour and sick-sweet, something had come up and grabbed him and dragged him down as he screamed and choked and fought to get away.

I leaned over the drain and called his name. My voice echoed, then stopped, like the Something had eaten the sound.

Then I heard the slurping echo up from the sewer.

# 5

I held the flashlight so tight that my fingers hurt. Was the slurping getting louder or not? I pointed the flashlight down into the sewer. A yellow dot of light bounced off something shiny.

Then the shiny Something moved, like a carpet crawling.

I yelled and backed up a step. My hands shook so hard I could hardly hold the flashlight. Then I smelled it. That sweet-sour smell that tasted like metal.

I turned and ran.

I forgot about Sheldon. I forgot about everything. I held the flashlight as tight as I could and just ran. I think I yelled again, but I didn't remember doing it. It just happened. So did the running. I ran so hard that I felt sick.

Something ran with me. It gurgled along, sucking along the road behind me. I gagged on the sweet-sour stink and ran faster.

When I got to school, I stopped. I leaned my hands on my knees and gulped down mouthfuls of air. The wind had wet my cheeks with tears from my eyes.

I had outrun it this time. But it seemed to be getting harder to do that.

I got to school so early that I had time to huddle out back and stop shaking all over. I looked at Sheldon's flashlight as I sat there.

*Why didn't you wait?*

I kept thinking that. Hadn't the light worked? Had he tried something to make it hot, or didn't any of it work? Had we been completely wrong about everything?

I kept seeing the flashlight in the gutter, the ants crawling all over it.

*Why didn't you wait?*

My "active-imagination" started being useful for once. Instead of seeing the ants on the flashlight, I saw Sheldon's ants—moving fast and poking around—as he fed them sugar-water. The ants on the flashlight ran around just like the ants in the jars had when Sheldon fed them.

I got up and walked over to Mrs. Ferman's classroom. Pressing my face up to the window with my hand over my eyes to block the light, I looked into the room at the jars.

What else goes on in summer, Sheldon had asked. I closed my eyes and summer came into my head.

Heat. Leaves rustling. The smell of cut grass. Long days. Lemonade. Long, hot days without a cloud in the sky. Birds. Ladybugs. Lots of other bugs.

And ants.

Ants everywhere. Mom scooping black trails

of them out of the kitchen. Ants swarming over the picnic food at the park. Ants pushing up piles of dirt all over the backyard.

I had to wait for Mrs. Ferman to open her classroom. Then I told her that Sheldon had said that I could take his ants home with me. She looked happy to get rid of them and even helped me stuff the flashlight into my back pocket and get both jars balanced in my arms.

It took me a long time to carry the jars to Fifth and Orchard. I was sweating by the time I got there. I put down the jars and looked at my watch. Half an hour until the late bell rang. For the first time, I hoped that I would get to school today.

Pulling Sheldon's flashlight from my back pocket, I turned it on.

No one had put the metal drain cover back on the sewer again. The sun was up now but not high enough to shine down into the sewer. I waited for the sun to come out from behind a cloud. Then I edged closer to the sewer.

That sweet-sour smell stayed in the air the way that Mom's cleaning stuff stays around for days after she does my room. Shining the light down, I saw what looked like a metal ladder on the wall. I went back for the ant jars. I took off my jacket and wrapped it around the jars. Then I tied the arms of my jacket around my waist so that it made a kind of backward backpack, with the jars sitting in front of me.

I sat on the pavement and let my feet dangle into the hole. I tried to imagine going down there and coming back up again. A stale smell came up at me.

Turning, I started to climb down into the sewer.

The jars banged against my chest as I climbed down. The metal felt cold and slick. I had to climb holding on with only one hand. My other hand held the flashlight. I kept the light pointed down and counted the steps.

One. I'm going to make it back.

Two. I'm going to find Sheldon.

Three. Four.

I slipped. One jar fell out of my make-do backpack. I heard it smash, the sound bouncing around in the sewer. I held the other jar to my side with my arm. I hung there, right foot kicking for the ladder. The other ant jar slipped around, and my fingers started to pull apart. Then my right toe found the next bar. I tried to pay more attention.

At the bottom, I took a deep breath and stepped off the ladder.

My feet squished into deep goo. The stuff oozed up over my shoes, turning them from white to instant brown. The smell almost made me sick. I got busy and untied my jacket sleeves and set the second ant jar down. I tried to swallow to get rid of the taste in my mouth.

It was dark. Almost as dark as night. I held my breath and listened. I could hear water or something dripping. The flashlight didn't give much light. The beam went out a few feet and then the darkness got too thick. The yellow glow jumped up and down. I put both my hands on the flashlight to make the glow stop jumping.

"Sheldon?" I called out, but not very loud.

I took a step forward. I stood in front of two tunnels, at the bottom of a Y. I took another step and slipped. Grabbing at the wall, I fell and the flashlight skidded out of my hand. I heard the second ant jar shatter as the flashlight smashed it. Then I landed on my rear in the goo. The flashlight hadn't broken, but now lay so that its light hit my face. It made it almost too bright for me to see. I put up a hand to shade my eyes.

The sound came from nowhere and everywhere. It sounded really close, almost in my ear. The hair tingled and stood up on my arms and neck. It sounded like someone dying.

I got to my feet, slipping and almost falling again. I couldn't see anything but colored dots dancing in the flashlight's yellow light. My hand closed on the ladder. Before I could think, I started climbing.

Halfway up, I remembered Sheldon.

I stopped climbing and hung there, holding the ladder tight. I felt like I would die if I let go. I looked up to see the round hole that led into daylight again. Go, just go, I kept thinking. Go. You don't have to stay. But I couldn't go. Not with Sheldon still down here.

I heard the moan again. Was it eating him? What was it doing to him? I knew that I had to find out or I would never sleep again.

Heart pounding, I started climbing down.

My hand shook as I picked up the flashlight.

I turned the light on the sewer again.

Green slime covered the walls. It dripped off the concrete in long, stringy bits. The stuff under my feet looked like chocolate pudding, but it didn't smell like it. The smell made me cough. I swung the light around. In the goo, I saw a banana peel half sticking up, spread out like octopus arms. I moved the light and a glow flashed off a tin can. I swung the light around again and spotted a twisted branch that stuck up out of the goo.

The beam of yellow flickered. I hit the side of the flashlight. When the beam came on again, it didn't look so bright. I hoped that Sheldon had put in fresh batteries this morning. I swung the beam of light around again.

The fading yellow beam made shadows across four glistening bumps. They had to be almost as big as I was. They didn't look like they belonged here. They didn't have sharp edges. They didn't have knobs or dials. They didn't look like anything someone would build for a sewer.

One of the bumps moved.

I froze, heart pounding. There it was, and it was moving, coming for me.

# 7

I couldn't move. I just stood there, staring at the bumps. Another one moved, wiggling like it was stuck. I squinted to see better and held up the flashlight.

It was stuck. All four of the bumps were stuck. They looked like the stuff a caterpillar puts around itself to make itself into a butterfly, except this stuff you could almost see through. Slowly, I eased forward.

I didn't want to touch the bumps, so I kept my hands back. But, when I was close enough, I pushed the flashlight up close to the nearest one.

Three or four feet high, maybe a little more, I guessed. It almost looked like the bump had something inside. I held the flashlight closer. I could almost see through to the center, but not quite. The stuff looked like the plastic Mom wraps around leftovers, only this stuff was inches thick.

Then I saw that the bump did have something inside.

It had Sheldon.

I slopped over to the branch and grabbed it

178

with one hand. Then I dragged it back to Sheldon. Setting the flashlight down on the goo so that the glow pointed at Sheldon, I stuck the branch into the stuff around him. I had to lean all my weight on it to make the branch slide in even just a little bit. A really awful smell came out and made me turn my face away. I pulled the stick out and the stuff closed over the hole again.

Then I remembered the ants.

I ran back to where the broken jars lay, slipping once in the goo and falling. I got up, covered now with goo, cold and shivering, my jeans and sweatshirt soaked with the awful-smelling stuff.

Ants swarmed out of the broken jars. Grabbing my jacket, I scooped some of the ant-jar dirt and the ants onto my jacket. The red ants stung my fingers. It felt like someone jabbing pins into my fingers. With both hands, I carried my jacket and the dirt back to the bump, and dumped it on top.

I went back for more dirt and ants. I dumped some of the ants on each wiggling bump. Then I picked up the flashlight and pushed it up so that I could see Sheldon again.

When I was little, before Robbie was born, Mom and Dad put in a videotape and showed me pictures of Robbie. The doctors used a special camera to film him. He hadn't looked like much, with his eyes closed, no hair and him wiggling around inside Mom. Sheldon looked like that now. Only he had hair and I could see his eyelashes.

The ants ate fast, digging into the stuff around Sheldon. They made tunnels in the stuff around Sheldon's head, and enough holes that I could stick my hand into the goo and pull it apart. It felt sticky, like glue, and it made my fingers numb. I pulled back from the stink as I stuck my hand in. Then I grabbed my jacket to wipe the stuff away from Sheldon's nose and eyes. He moaned, and I heard something else. Something from one of the sewer tunnels.

I started working faster and shaking Sheldon's shoulder to wake him. "Sheldon! Sheldon! Get up. Come on!"

His eyes opened. Then his mouth opened to scream. I stuffed my hand across his mouth. "No! Don't do that. We have to get out of here." I got the rest of the goo off his shoulders and arms. He wasn't wearing his jacket, but as I scraped the stuff off his chest, a long metal zipper fell down in the goo. I hadn't time to wonder where it came from. I just kept scraping.

"Come on," I said, hands still shaking. "We have to get the others out."

Sheldon nodded like he had just got out of bed and wasn't really awake. He stumbled out of the goo, his legs making sucking sounds as he pulled free. He had trouble standing and I grabbed his arms to help him.

I could smell it now, that sick-sweet smell like watermelon-sours and rotten eggs. The metallic taste on my tongue. Sheldon looked really pale in the yellow glow of the flashlight. I worried that he might be sick on me, but he started helping to get the others out of the stuff around them.

We got the little girl out first. The ants had eaten a lot of the goo around her. But she acted like she didn't want to wake up. Her eyes kept closing. Then her head would fall back like she was just a stuffed doll. I left Sheldon trying to get her awake and I got the boy with the short hair loose.

The slurping sound got louder. It sounded like it was just down the tunnel. It sounded like all it had to do was slide over a few feet and it could cover all of us again. Who would find us then?

Who would know to look down here for us?

It wasn't moving fast, but maybe it didn't need to. Maybe it got lazy like the way I felt after one of Mom's big family dinners. Or maybe it just liked waiting a little and making us sweat a lot.

"Hurry," I hissed at Sheldon. "Get the girl out." She had started to wake up and cry. The short-haired boy had his eyes open, but he couldn't move too well. His arms and hands kind of flopped. It might have been funny any other time and place.

The third lump turned out to be the other missing kid, a dark-skinned boy with straight black hair like mine. As I helped him pull his feet out of the goo, I saw that he didn't have any bottoms on his shoes, just laces and tops. He started punching at me as he started waking up. I had to get Sheldon to help me hold him while we got him on his feet and walking.

By the time the last kid stumbled over to the ladder, the sound had moved real close. I was afraid we weren't going to make it. Not all of us. The girl stumbled around the way Robbie does when he's walking in his sleep. The two boys and Sheldon were doing better, but climbing that ladder would be hard. And we had to go up one at a time.

I grabbed the flashlight and swung it around to shine on the broken ant jars. All I saw was two piles of dirt and broken glass. The ants had crawled away. I swung the light around to the ladder.

The girl was almost at the top. The boy with the dark hair crowded after her. The other boy had already got out. That left Sheldon—and me. I looked and noticed again that the boy with the dark hair didn't have any bottoms on his shoes. I remembered the zipper falling off Sheldon, but without a jacket. I grabbed Sheldon's arm.

"What's plastic made from?"

He blinked at me, then pushed his glasses to straighten them. "Made from?"

"Your jacket, it was made out of some kind of plastic, wasn't it?" That sour-sweet smell was getting stronger. "Was the plastic made from oil?" I yelled at him.

Sheldon nodded, then started climbing.

I turned around and pulled off my sneakers. Mom had gotten them on sale so she wouldn't be too mad if I lost them. They were cheap plastic, like Sheldon's jacket. I threw them as far as I could, one down each tunnel. Maybe that would keep it busy. I looked at the flashlight. It was plastic. I threw it, too. It thunked into a wall and the yellow glow went out.

I started to climb up after Sheldon.

My feet slipped. I could hardly grip the metal. My fingers felt as sleepy as Sheldon looked. I knew it was from that stuff that had been around the other kids. I climbed faster, hooking my arms around the ladder sides to hang on. At every step, I heard it moving behind me, creeping closer. The smell was everywhere.

I could see the round O of light ahead. Sheldon had made it out. Everyone had made it out. Everyone except me.

I was reaching for the top ladder bar when something wrapped around my ankle.

I screamed. I screamed Sheldon's name and I just plain screamed. I tried to shake loose, only I couldn't. It pulled and my other foot slipped off the ladder. I hung on, arms locked. It pulled and I fell back an inch.

"Sheldon! It's got me! Sheldon!" I yelled. My voice bounced off the walls around me. He must have heard me. Why didn't he do something? Was he still too sleepy?

It pulled again, tugging the way Robbie pulls on me when he wants something and is afraid to ask. It felt like something was testing to see how hard it really had to pull to get me loose.

My arms slipped away from the ladder. I wrapped numb fingers around the cold metal. Slowly, my fingers started working loose. I knew that I couldn't hang on much longer.

"Sheldon!"

Something hit me on the head.

I looked up in time to see a plastic bucket with a hole in it falling at me. I twisted. The bucket hit my shoulder and bounced off. My left hand came off the ladder. I hung from my right hand.

"Move away," Sheldon yelled.

I looked up and saw him staring down.

"I can't!" I yelled, my throat sore from screaming.

A big plastic milk carton fell down next and hit me on the shoulder. I started screaming again.

Then it let go.

I swung from my one hand, feeling like one of the tetherballs on the school playground. Only I didn't have a chain holding me to anything. I had four fingers I could hardly feel and a single thumb about to pop off.

I couldn't reach up to grab the ladder. Kicking my legs, I tried to swing around. When would it fill up on the other stuff and come grab me again?

Then I felt someone's hand on my wrist.

I looked up. Sheldon's head and arms dangled into the sewer. "Grab hold!" he yelled.

Kicking again, I swung around. He grabbed my left hand just as my right lost its grip on the ladder. Both his hands came around my left wrist. I felt wetness on my face and knew that I must be crying. I didn't care if I was. I just wanted out.

"Pull us up," Sheldon called, twisting around to the circle of light above him.

Sheldon started going up and I went with him. I heard the thing slurping behind us. It's getting ready to come up, I thought.

Then we were out in daylight.

I lay on the road, the breath hurting in my chest. In daylight, the other kids looked pale, like they had been sick for a long time. They sat around a pile of junk, stuff they had raided from every trash can on the street—broken plastic lamps, bits of grocery bags, big soda pop bottles.

Then I heard it slurping up the sewer, dripping stuff, smelling as it came.

"We're not safe yet. Come on!" Pushing up, I got to my feet and stubbed my toe. The dark-haired boy started to grab some of the junk. I grabbed his arm. "Leave it! We've got to find some ants!"

Stumbling, we sort of ran. We spent more time tripping on our feet, falling, and skinning our knees and hands than anything. The smell followed and fell around us. And the slurping sound came with it, louder than ever.

When we got to the house on the corner, we had to stop. The little girl started crying again and couldn't run anymore. The two other boys fell onto the grass, their chests going up and down in fast motion.

I looked at Sheldon. "We made it bigger by feeding it."

He nodded. We both turned.

"It's coming up again," he said, his voice really quiet.

I grabbed his arm. "Where'd you get your

ants? Where did they come from?"

He pointed to the empty lot where I had first seen him sitting.

I had to cross the street to get there.

"Get the others as far away as you can," I shouted, already running.

The rocks on the street hurt my feet, making me hop and say words that Mom doesn't like me saying. Looking back, I saw Sheldon help the short-haired boy get up. They got the girl up and all of them started moving down Orchard. How far away was safe enough? I didn't know.

I found an anthill near one of the metal boxes, right in the middle of the empty lot. I looked around. I didn't have anything to dig up the ants with. I swung around. If I couldn't get the ants to it, I could do something else.

I stood beside the anthill, hopping from one foot to the other, shaking my numb hands and wishing Sheldon had been more awake so that he could be here instead of me. He was the brave one. I was just the stupid one to be here. But he and the others couldn't run anymore. They needed time to get away.

My mind played pictures of the others under all that goo. Something wanted me stuck down in the sewer in that weird sleep. Stuck there forever. I got mad. It just ate stuff. What it didn't eat, it wrapped up and just held on to. I got even madder. Suddenly I wanted really badly to make that thing smaller. After all it had done, I was mad at it. I wanted it gone.

It oozed up like a toilet overflowing. Black, sparkling inside, colors swirling like an oil slick, it sucked ahead. It rolled out, spilling forward. Then it would hump up, arching like it had a back and spine. Only it didn't. It was only goo. It was thousands, maybe gazillions of those microbe-things that ate plastic. Plastic made of oil. Just like that article in the library had said. In the summer, ants swarmed up out of their holes and ate the sweet-sick goo. Then, when it got cold and rainy, the ants were deep in the dirt, and it got the chance to eat—and get bigger again.

"Come and get me!" I yelled. It stopped as if it had heard. "Come on, you slime-pit! Come on, you stinking pool of crude. Come and eat this!"

Lifting up, it rose into the air and spread itself out so that it looked like it could fly. It moved faster than I thought it could. Faster than I could ever run. I held my breath and stumbled back. Then I got angry again. I stepped forward, hands clenched in fists and my face hot.

"Yeah, over here, slime sucker! Come on, garbage-stink! Come get me!"

It fell like night around me. I looked up and it filled the sky. I stumbled backward, fell and crawled. It slapped onto my face, wet and numbing, and onto my shoulders and my arms and my legs.

I woke up as something stung me. Small, pinching stings, like needles poking me all over. I blinked my eyes open. I saw sky—beautiful, cloudy, gray sky. I raised my head.

I had been dragged onto the sidewalk. My socks stuck into the street. And I had ants all over me. Big, red, stinging ants that left spots every time they pinched.

"Ouch!" I almost slapped at one on my arm. Then I remembered the goo falling over me and I left the ant alone. It had helped save my life.

Ants swarmed over every pebble and rock. Thick lines of them headed out to the sewer drains. I laughed, but it made my sides hurt. Brushing at the ants, I got up. I felt sore everywhere. My face felt numb. It was great to still be able to feel at all.

I wasn't sure it was gone. Maybe the ants had only made it go back. Maybe they had just made it a lot smaller. Maybe. I wasn't going to take any chances.

Mom calls me her "eco-warrior" now. I'm not sure that's any better than having an "active imagination." It sounds better, but I'm not sure it is. I got an idea that day the thing almost got me about how we could get rid of it. We, Sheldon and I and the other kids, started this group to stop people from dumping stuff down the sewer drain. Especially anything with oil in it.

Having an "active imagination" also helped a lot when Sheldon and I had to explain how we found the missing kids. We nearly got into trouble over that. Everyone seemed to think we were lying when we told the truth. So I got Sheldon to get the other kids to stay quiet, and I started talking.

I don't know where the story came from, it just came out, about finding the kids tied up in this warehouse. I even found a warehouse that I could point out to the police as the one where we found them. After that, Mom, Dad, and Robbie and Sheldon's parents seemed to think we were heroes.

That helped a lot when we started our drain-watch group.

Sheldon even thinks it's working. It's summer now so it's hard to tell. But I haven't seen any other kids show up on the milk cartons as missing on Fifth and Orchard. And the anthill on the empty lot near Fifth and Orchard looks bigger than ever this year.